"Can I work here, too? As a live-in staff member ...?"

Rit
(Rizlet of Loggervia)

The princess of the Duchy of Loggervia. Has adventured with Red's party in the past. One thing led to another, and she forced herself into Red's shop and is now living with him. An easily embarrassed girl who has outgrown her more combative phase.

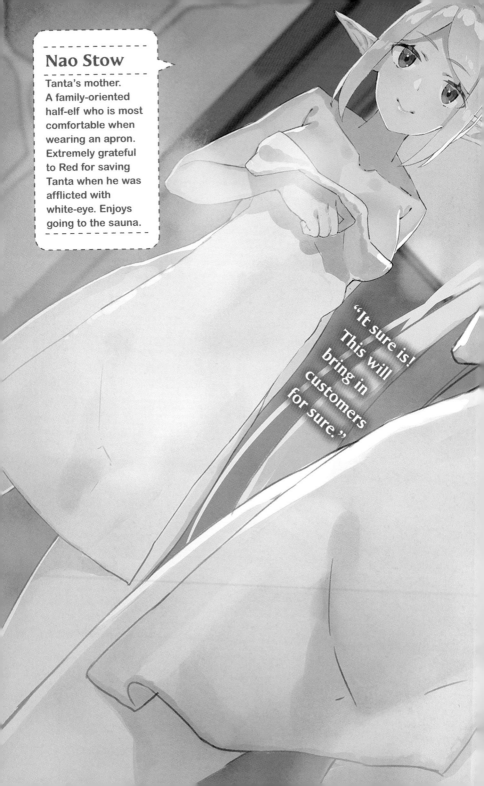

"Waaaah, it really is a lovely fragrance."

Red
(Gideon Ragnason)
Has the initial skill "level +30" but was pushed out of the Hero's party when the others finally surpassed his level. He headed to the frontier to live a slow life.

Apparently, news of the medicine spread quickly by word of mouth. Before nightfall, several customers had stopped in to buy some medicinal cookies.

Danan LeBeau

A big, brawny man with the divine blessing of the Martial Artist. Used to be the master of a dojo in a town that was destroyed by the demon lord's army. Despite this, there is no trace of that dark past in his hearty personality.

Yarandrala

A high elf with the divine blessing of the Singer of the Trees. She is capable of controlling plants. Became a member of the Hero's party during the battle in Loggervia. Among her companions, Red was the one she trusted the most, but...

Theodora Dephilo

The pinnacle of human clerics and assistant instructor of the temple knight's style of spear wielding. Bearer of the divine blessing of the Crusader. A warrior at heart, she has a stoic personality. Has a high opinion of Red's abilities.

Ares Srowa

Bearer of the divine blessing of the Sage, greatest of the mage blessings. The man who pushed Red out of the party. Son of a failed duke, he joined the Hero's party in order to restore his family's power.

Ruti Ragnason

Red's younger sister and possessor of the divine blessing of the Hero, humanity's strongest blessing. She was extremely attached to her big brother and always clung to him when the two were younger. Before he left the party, Red used to dote on his cute little sister.

Albert Leland

The frontier's strongest adventurer. Has the divine blessing of the Champion and a strong ambition to move up in the world. Although in the top tier for the frontier, he only ended up drifting out to Zoltan after not being able to cut it in Central.

Stormthunder

A half-orc who runs a furniture business in the blue-collar part of town where Red lives. A stubborn, working-class craftsman, he rolls out a rarely seen businessman's smile when customers with money to spend stop by.

Newman Winters

The trusty doctor in Red's working-class part of town. Became close with Red when he was taking care of Tanta's white-eye. One of Red's regular clients.

Tanta Stow

A young half-elf boy who gets on well with Red. Was in danger of going blind due to white-eye, but Red cured him. His dream is to become a carpenter.

I Decided to Live a Quiet Life in the Countryside

1

ZAPPON

Illustration by
Yasumo

YEN ON

New York

Banished from the Hero's Party, I Decided to Live a Quiet Life in the Countryside, Vol. 1
Zappon

Translation by Dale DeLucia
Cover art by Yasumo

▼ ▼

SHIN NO NAKAMA JYANAI TO YUUSHA NO PARTY WO OIDASARETANODE, HENKYOU DE SLOW—LIFE SURUKOTO NI SHIMASHITA Vol. 1
©Zappon, Yasumo 2018
First published in Japan in 2018 by KADOKAWA CORPORATION, Tokyo.
English translation rights arranged with KADOKAWA CORPORATION, Tokyo through TUTTLE-MORI AGENCY, INC., Tokyo.

English translation © 2020 by Yen Press, LLC

Yen On
150 West 30th Street, 19th Floor
New York, NY 10001

Visit us at yenpress.com
facebook.com/yenpress
twitter.com/yenpress
yenpress.tumblr.com
instagram.com/yenpress

First Yen On Edition: September 2020

Yen On is an imprint of Yen Press, LLC.
The Yen On name and logo are trademarks of Yen Press, LLC.

▼ ▼

Library of Congress Cataloging-in-Publication Data
Names: Zappon, author. | Yasumo, illustrator. | DeLucia, Dale, translator.
Title: Banished from the hero's party, I decided to live a quiet life in the countryside / Zappon ; illustration by Yasumo ; translation by Dale DeLucia ; cover art by Yasumo.
Other titles: Shin no nakama ja nai to yuusha no party wo oidasareta node, henkyou de slow life suru koto ni shimashita. English
Description: First Yen On edition. | New York : Yen On, 2020.
Identifiers: LCCN 2020026847 | ISBN 9781975312459 (v. 1 ; trade paperback)
Subjects: CYAC: Ability—Fiction. | Fantasy.
Classification: LCC PZ7.1.Z37 Ban 2020 | DDC [Fic]—dc23
LC record available at https://lccn.loc.gov/2020026847

ISBNs: 978-1-9753-1245-9 (paperback)
978-1-9753-1246-6 (ebook)

1 3 5 7 9 10 8 6 4 2

LSC-C

Printed in the United States of America

CONTENTS

Illustration: Yasumo
Design Work: Shindousha

Prologue

- - - - - - - - -

Setting Off

The Hero's village was consumed in flames. Orcs with tusks protruding from their mouths like wild boars were waving sabers with one hand while gripping what little there was to pillage with their other. The creatures bellowed fearsome roars.

The Hero, who had lived a life entirely disconnected from fighting until this day, readied a cheap bronze sword from her house in one hand and faced down three orcs.

"...!"

But she did not cut a very reassuring image compared to her powerful-looking opponents. Even the Hero, who bore the potential to become the most powerful being someday, was—at this point—still just a young girl who knew nothing of battle.

The struggle was decided quickly. The Hero's strike left a shallow cut in one of the orc's arms, but she was quickly caught in a grapple from behind by one of its brethren. An orc's muscular hand clamped down on the wrist of her hand grasping the sword, and the girl was immobilized.

The Hero struggled desperately, but her defiance merely amused the orcs. One of the creatures licked his lips all the way up one of his tusks with a long red tongue as a coarse grin twisted his fearsome face. The brute's gnarled hand reached out to touch the Hero.

However, the orc's hand froze as it closed on empty air.

"Huh?"

The monster felt a burning heat at his back and tilted his head in wonder. He tried to turn around but was hit by a sudden sense of exhaustion and dropped to his knees, promptly collapsing.

* * *

My mithril spear smoothly pierced the orc's back, and he slumped, unmoving. His companions saw me riding my drake with a spear in hand. Their eyes were drawn to the dragon crest adorning the chest plate of my armor.

"The crest of the Bahamut Knights?! What's a knight from the capital doing in a backwater village like this?!"

The orcs screamed in fear. They'd likely planned to just ransack a helpless little village but instead now faced a drake knight from the capital of the kingdom, one of the elites of the Bahamut Knights, feared even among the ranks of the demon lord's armies.

"Gyah!"

While the brutish raiders were distracted by shock, the Hero kicked the shin of the orc holding her and freed her sword arm. A smile crossed the Hero's face as she ran toward me.

I leaped down from my drake, set aside my spear, and drew my blade as I stood in the orcs' path, shielding my little sister, the Hero.

"You dared to lay your hands on my little sister. I hope you're ready for the consequences," I said as I rushed into the orcs with my knight's sword.

This was the first page of the Hero's story. The Hero defeated the creatures attacking her hometown, allowing the villagers time to escape. Those orcs turned out to be advance troops from the demon lord's army. While they were taking control of the surrounding villages one after the other, the Hero became the pillar of the resistance. She saved those wronged by the evil forces and raised the signal for all the gathered people to strike back against the demon lord.

Chapter 1

- - - - - - - - -

Apparently, I Wasn't a True Comrade

It had been three years since Taraxon, the Raging Demon Lord—ruler of the dark continent—began an invasion of the continent of Avalon.

In just three years, four different countries had been destroyed, and half of Avalon had fallen into the demon lord's hands. But just when the people began to despair that they could do nothing to stop the destruction…it turned out that the god of their world had not abandoned them.

The Hero's birth was prophesied. And then a girl suddenly took command of forces in the countryside that should have had hardly any soldiers with combat experience and managed to beat back the demon lord's army's advance forces. The Hero, Ruti Ragnason, appeared in the capital bearing proof of the Divine Blessing of the Hero. Evidence that anyone would recognize and accept. From arranging a compromise to stopping the fighting with an underground band of thieves in the capital to recovering the proof of the Hero that was resting in ruins from the ancient time of the elves to various feats beyond, the girl's exploits convinced the king that she was indeed who she claimed to be.

And thus, the Hero set off on a journey to save the world, accompanied by the cheers and blessings of the people.

✳   ✳   ✳

Zoltan. The frontier.

Far from the Hero's hometown, Zoltan was on the front lines of the war with the demon lord's army. Blessed with a wealth of rivers—but in the path of storms coming out of the southern ocean. Protected to the north and east by the vast, unexplored mountain range known as the Wall at the End of the World. Covered in wetlands, so transportation and communication were difficult, hardly having developed at all. It was a land with no strategic value.

With its bounty of rivers and the replenishment of nutrients that came from storms that caused the rivers to overflow, one could make a decent living just spreading seeds around farmland with good drainage. But of those who seriously devoted themselves to agriculture there, many lost everything to the squalls that blew it all away. As a result, the people developed a natural laziness and distaste for hard work.

People working in Central were all scared of the threat of being demoted and sent to the lazy land of Zoltan. Even criminals who preyed on various villages left Zoltan alone because they knew they couldn't make a living here. The only travelers who came to the frontier were fugitives, hermits, or eccentrics.

But as I was now, this sort of place suits me.

"Three kilos of nightshade, two kilos of koku leaves, one bag of white berries..."

I placed the medicinal herbs I had gathered on the table at the Adventurers Guild's collection desk.

"Thanks for all your hard work, Red... Your total comes out to one hundred and thirty payril."

The girl at the counter promptly breezed through the calculations and handed over silver payril coins for my payment.

"We look forward to working with you again."

Seeing me leave the counter, the other adventurers all grinned.

"Hey, Red, still gathering medicinal herbs? How 'bout spicing things up a bit with a goblin extermination for a change?"

"Sorry, this is a bit more my speed."

"Come on, man—that bronze sword of yours is seriously lame. An adventurer who doesn't even have at least an iron sword is an embarrassment to the job."

I just shrugged. It's not as if I particularly liked being made fun of, but compared to how things used to be, this was nothing.

These guys were just shooting the breeze; they weren't serious. They had the same lazy Zoltan spirit as everyone else and stuck to taking easy quests.

As for why I was working as an adventurer in a place like this... That's a story from before I became a specialist in herb collection.

✳   ✳   ✳

In the past—though it was less than a year ago—I was a member of Ruti the Hero's party.

At the time, my name was Gideon Ragnason. To be frank, the Hero—Ruti Ragnason—is my little sister.

In this world, people receive a Divine Blessing when they are born. It's considered a gift from God in order to guide people down the paths they should live. They're granted strengths appropriate to that path, which is why they are called Divine Blessings. Power could also be granted in the form of skills based on what kind of blessing you have. Those with blessings in the Warrior or Mage trees could take on warrior or mage skills.

My blessing was Guide, one that had never been seen before. The power it granted was an initial blessing of level +30. I was born at level 31. I had a level equivalent to a knight in the royal guard. It caused a pretty big fuss at first. By the time I was six, I was heading out to exterminate monsters, and by eight, I was recruited into the knighthood. At seventeen, I had already risen to second-in-command.

When it came out that my little sister was the Hero, we started getting praised as the twin hopes of humanity. When Ruti and I returned from skirmishes in the countryside, Ruti was finally recognized by the king as the Hero, and when she set out from the capital to defeat the demon lord, I was obviously added to the party.

At that point, I was stronger than my sister and was one of the top five knights in the capital. No one opposed me joining the Hero's party.

No one except the Sage, Ares, another member of our group.

In the end, Ares was right.

My blessing, Guide, was a power meant only to protect the beginning of the Hero's journey. As everyone else's levels rose, they learned powerful new skills, and the limitation of the Guide's blessing became apparent.

With the Hero's blessing, hero skills could be used; with the Sage's blessing, sage skills could be used; with Warrior-style blessings, all sorts of warrior skills could be used... But there were no guide skills.

The only ones I could choose were common abilities anyone could learn. When we set out, I was strong relative to the rest of the group. Over time, however, they caught up to and eventually surpassed me. Gradually, I became deadweight. My role was that of the party member who helped the immature Hero in the early stages only to drop out midway through the quest.

*   *   *

"You are not a true comrade."

That was what the Sage, Ares, told me when we were headed to the local lord's mansion to celebrate after the intense battle with Desmond of the Earth, one of the four heavenly kings of the demon lord's army.

"What do you mean?"

"A true comrade is someone who fulfills their role. Someone with whom you can fight back-to-back."

"And you're saying I'm not that?"

"Surely you've noticed it by now, right? To be succinct, you're a liability. During the fight with Desmond of the Earth, what did you do?"

"...I fought with my sword."

"No, your sword didn't deal any noticeable damage to Desmond. In fact, Desmond was probably just completely ignoring you. You got caught up in some of the area of effect attacks, but there wasn't a single strike actually aimed at you."

That was certainly true. Desmond had definitely been ignoring me.

"You were judged to not be a threat. And yet you still failed to escape the area of effect attacks where you weren't even the target. What's worse, if you get hurt, Ruti will make me heal and protect you. For no reason other than that, I am forced to waste my spells."

"That's..."

"You're not even just a liability. Your very existence is a weight holding Ruti back."

"It's not like I'm not trying my best to be helpful."

"Trying your best? Are you an idiot?"

"What?!"

"Trying your best is an explanation for success, but it does not excuse being a liability. You think you can be forgiven for holding us back just because you're trying your best? How selfish can you be?! You really aren't a true member of the party!"

I was speechless.

Now might really be the time, I thought. The thing I had always been considering... This seemed like the moment for it.

"But I'm the second-in-command of the Bahamut Knights; if I return to them being labeled a liability, it would be a stain upon their honor..."

"Faced with a threat to the world, you would worry about the honor of the knights?"

"Tell the others... Tell them I went on my own to scout the situation with the demon lord's army...and never came back. Can you tell them that for me?"

"I see. Very well, then. We can go with that story."

"...Thanks."

My head downward, I started to leave.

"Hey." Ares stopped me. "Leave your equipment. We're the ones who earned that."

"..."

The treasure sword Thunderwaker, a mental-defense ring, a cloak of evasion, and more. I removed all my equipment. In exchange, I took a little bit of money for the road and a cheap bronze sword from Ares and departed.

Still, I had some lingering attachment. The next day, before leaving, I wanted to see my little sister's face one last time. She had always been so fond of me, always calling me Big Brother.

Of course, she was way stronger than me by then, but still, when I thought of her going off by herself from then on, I got worried. Also...I kind of hoped she would be a little upset about me leaving. But...when I peeked stealthily through a window, I was greeted by the image of Ares with his arm around that same little sister's shoulder.

"Oh...so that's how it was...?"

She didn't need me anymore. That was perfectly clear. Just like the Sage had said, I wasn't a real comrade. Dammit. The thought of it is still hard to bear. I kept pitifully muttering to myself "I know you don't need your big brother anymore, but I hope you still remember me from time to time" as I left town that morning.

From there, I changed my name to Red. I wandered, eventually settling in this forsaken land. Now I make a living as a boring adventurer who specializes in herb gathering.

✳ ✳ ✳

"It was really rough back then."

After ending up all alone like that, I bawled my eyes out for a bit. Being pushed out of the party left me too dejected to do anything else for a while. I half-heartedly beat up a group of thieves that was causing a fuss near the town where I was staying and stole their money. I spent the lot of it on booze. I'd never really been a drinker before, but I got blind drunk while trying to forget my problems. Unfortunately, that started to attract attention.

If anyone figured out my identity, it would surely be a big problem for the knight captain and the head of the territory who had done so much to support me. So I pulled myself up and ventured out to the frontier under the assumed identity of an adventurer named Red. There, I found a new dream for myself, a new way to live.

"I'm going to open an apothecary here in Zoltan and live a comfortable, easy, slow life! I don't have any talent for battle, so I'm going to live peacefully from now on!"

I was still worried about my sister, but as I was far weaker than her, there wasn't much I could do even if I fretted over her every day. I wasn't even a real comrade, so I decided to leave the demon lord to them and just live for myself!

To that end, I started saving money from medicinal-herb-gathering jobs while drawing up a map of the distribution of medicinal herbs by season, in preparation for my future.

✳   ✳   ✳

You might find yourself wondering if perhaps there's some kind of hidden super-cheat to the Guide blessing. Nope. There isn't.

Blessings give both an initial skill and innate skills that are unlocked upon leveling up. There are also common skills that can be taken anytime.

A guide's initial skill provides a starter blessing of level +30. An incredibly powerful ability. Blessing level 30 was around where your average knight might be when retiring from duty. I started at a level that someone else might spend his or her whole life trying to achieve. But I had no innate skills to choose. All there is to the ability is just being reasonably strong at the outset. Even if someone wanted to take advantage of that initial skill, there was no room for broad improvement. A person without skills was significantly weaker than someone at the same level with skills. If you wanted to fight in order to raise your blessing level and earn skill points to get stronger, you wouldn't be able to beat enemies that another person at the same level would be able to handily dispatch. That meant you'd have to defeat people with lower blessing levels than you, which was significantly less efficient. Thinking about it, it was hardly a blessing at all. Even blessings like Warrior or Mage—with their abundance of skills—might've been better, despite being considered lower tier. At least they had room for growth.

So with my heart broken, I set my sight on a slow life and gradually earning money.

I headed into the mountains again to gather some more herbs today.

Since I have a high level but innate skills to acquire, I've assembled a decent collection of common skills. Thanks to the Survival skill, as long as I don't go too deep into the woods while hiking, I won't get lost. Plus, I can recognize the standard medicinal herbs one can gather. It's just a common skill, though, so it only covers the spectrum of standard plants.

"Henbane is an antiseptic and hemostatic to stop bleeding, koku leaves are for antidotes, ryujin mushrooms are immune-system-boosting nutritional supplements, and rare white berries can be catalysts for magic potions."

I hummed to myself as I diligently scavenged the herbs for the day. In Zoltan, with its abundance of water and pretty much nothing else, the mountains could be called a natural storehouse containing a bounty of medicinal herbs and fruits.

"Oh, green nuts. I can boil those for dinner when I make camp."

Generally, herb gathering was a two-day, one-night trip. Because it took about half a day's travel, it wasn't very efficient to return the same day. I was used to camping from all the time I spent traveling anyway. I would find non-medicinal herbs and wild plants to cook while I was out.

"But it's definitely a bit tiresome to camp out in the middle of the mountains."

Monsters weren't scared of fire. I slept with my sword next to me and a rope attached to a strung-up bell for a little peace of mind. There weren't any particularly dangerous monsters around here, but it was still possible to get attacked in my sleep and suffer an unexpected injury.

"Ahhh, maybe I should make a little lodge here soon."

The people living in the area hadn't built a mountain cabin because they figured it would just get destroyed by a storm before long, but its construction wouldn't have to be that great to withstand the wind and rain. It only needed to be sturdy enough that monsters would have to exert a bit of an effort to knock it down.

Lately, I've been coming here twice a week to gather medicinal herbs, so it would be way easier to just make it a four-day, three-night trip. But in order to stay in the mountains that long, I would need a place to put my bags and rest, which would mean I'd need a little hut or something.

"Well, I can deal with that after I've saved up a bit more money."

I drifted off to sleep with thoughts of my future aspirations.

I woke up during the night. There was a gamey scent in the distance accompanied by the presence of a large animal.

I silently drew my sword close as I studied the interloper. Even though I didn't have any special skills to enhance my senses like someone with a Thief or Hunter blessing, my Sense skill's level was high, since there was nothing else to spend my skill points on.

It wouldn't be enough for something like the demon lord's elite ninja squad, but it was more than sufficient to perceive a monster dwelling in these mountains.

There didn't seem to be any sign of it approaching soon, so I got out of my sleeping bag and silently climbed a tree. A crescent moon like a tightly drawn bow hung in the starry sky. Its pale light wasn't bright enough for me to catch sight of the creature, however. After peering for a while, I heard a bell ring. A large beast's face emerged from the darkness.

"Oh, an owlbear?"

As the name implied, an owlbear was a magic beast with an owl's head and brown bear's body. Generally, owlbears were monsters around level 15. They were common magic beasts that lived in forests around the world. Fairly apex predators, they lived as the free-spirited kings of their forests. How nostalgic. I'd fought one of these before. That must've been back when I chased after Ruti, who'd gone charging into the forest looking for some friends of hers who'd gotten lost.

That was around when I was seven. Nowadays, I could easily handle one, but...

"Well, it's not like there's a reward for it."

I nimbly hopped down from the tree. Animals and low-intelligence monsters like magic beasts could instinctually sense when their opponent was stronger. The owlbear and I exchanged glances before it slowly moved back, turned around, and ran off into the dark of the woods. I didn't bother chasing after it and just climbed back into my sleeping bag and slept until morning.

*   *   *

The next day, after I'd finished gathering what I needed, I returned to town to find it in an uproar for some reason. I tried asking the guard at the gate if anything had happened.

"What's up?"

"Oh, Red, you staying safe?"

"Yeah, same as always. Things seem a bit troubled here, though. Something happen?"

"There were some adventurers who got attacked by an owlbear. They're currently trying to put together a group to go take care of it, so the mountains will probably be off-limits until it's been sorted."

Oops. That owlbear had probably stumbled across me after attacking some adventurers nearby.

"Really? How long do you think it'll take?"

"Who knows. It's pretty rare to have something as big as an owlbear show up around here. It'll probably be either our ace B-rank party or else a big group of thirty some odd people."

Adventurers are categorized into six ranks from S down to E. The ranks are based on parties rather than individuals, so when the makeup of the party changes, so, too, does its rank. Generally speaking:

> E: Rookies who just registered
> D: A party that can survive in the wild where monsters roam
> C: A party that can resolve a crisis that endangers a village
> B: A party that can resolve a crisis that endangers a town
> A: A country-level party that can resolve a crisis that involves multiple cities
> S: A legendary-class party that is mobilized to deal with crises threatening a continent or the world

Generally speaking, most towns have around one to three B-rank parties that form the peak of the local power-dynamic pyramid. Only really big cities like the kingdom's capital would have an A-rank party. Right now, all the best adventurers were active on the front lines fighting the demon lord's army.

Incidentally, I'm D rank. It can't really be helped, since I basically just collect herbs, and if I ended up rising to B rank here, I'd stand out too much and people might figure out who I was. Worst-case scenario, if that happened, it would cause problems for the head of the knights, my benefactor. As such, I was content leaving the owlbear to other adventurers.

"I guess I'll have to sit tight in town for a while."
At least I was able to finish my business in the mountains first. I headed to the Adventurers Guild to sell my wares.

*   *   *

My earnings this time totaled around ninety payril.

After returning to my room in the town house where I was living, I did the regular maintenance on my bronze sword, though I had only been using it to cut plants lately. I also repaired my traveling clothes that had gotten torn up from hiking.

I had raised my Repair skill a fair amount. Back when we were fighting on the frontier, before we'd set out for the capital, it had proved pretty useful. As time went on, though, everything became reparable via magic, so it had become redundant along the way. But I didn't have any mage acquaintances now who could use Repair magic, and armorers cost money. Since I was saving to open my own apothecary, it was definitely a valuable skill.

Having finished the upkeep of my gear, I used some eggs and potatoes from my pantry and the green nuts I brought back from the mountains to make a dinner of salad and mashed potatoes.

When that was done, I used the shared washroom to rinse myself off and went to bed.

This wasn't some battlefield with monster corpses strewn everywhere, a dragon's nest with scores of the creatures, or a frozen snowy mountain. It was just a small room with a roof, so I could close my eyes in peace.

Once I saved up enough money, I would build my own house and operate the apothecary from it. I'd set up a garden in the back to cultivate some of the more important medicinal herbs, too. It wouldn't be some huge success, but there wouldn't be any life-or-death battles or nerve-racking conspiracies to deal with. That was the sort of life that could be had here in Zoltan.

This was my second chance after getting pushed out of the Hero's party.

* * * * * *

Three days later, a team of twenty-seven adventurers was assembled to hunt down the owlbear, and they ventured off into the mountains bolstered by cheers from the townsfolk at their backs. During that time, I was fishing at a nearby river and selling what I caught.

The work earned me eight payril. It was possible to get a room and two meals a day for only one, so eight payril for three days' effort was a decent haul. In order to open my own apothecary, though, I would need 1,730 in funds.

I was gradually saving up, but between the general cost of living, buying preserved rations in order to go out to the mountains to gather herbs, and maintaining my gear, my actual profit for a single trip was only about thirty payril. At that rate, I was going to have to keep doing this for another six months.

"Well, not that that's the end of the world."

There was no particular rush. No impending peril loomed, so I could just take my time.

I was lying on my bed and reading a book I'd borrowed from the library to kill some time. It was shortly after noon when I heard a knock on the thin door to my town house.

"Coming." I tucked a bookmark between the pages and hung my bronze sword from the belt at my waist as I headed to the entrance. Readying my sword was a habit I had picked up from my old quests.

There had been several occasions when we'd been attacked in our sleep back in those days. The experience made it tough to sleep if I wasn't ready to fight at a moment's notice. Even after I was ousted, I still wasn't really comfortable turning in without a weapon close at hand. It felt weird to be unarmed when a gust of wind blew by, too.

Living the slow life meant I would need to do something about those habits, though...

"Who is it?"

I opened the door to see Megria, one of the employees of the Adventurers Guild. Behind her stood a man wearing fancy-looking armor along with what was clearly his party.

"I'm sorry to bother you while you're resting, Red."

"Oh, Megria. What is it? And Albert, too." The armored man, Albert, twitched at the offhand greeting.

"Show some respect, D rank."

Albert was one of only two B-rank adventurers in town. There were no higher-ranking adventurers, and the other B rank, Rit, only worked solo. Thus, Albert's party was considered the ace team of the Adventurers Guild in these parts.

"...Right, Albert, sir. So what brings you here?"

Albert moved toward me, beaming as he patted me on the shoulder.

"I've heard stories about you. You specialize in gathering medicinal herbs and know more about the mountains than anyone, yes?"

"I do my best."

"My party is headed to take out the owlbear. It's not something we would normally handle, but the first suppression team failed, so there's no one else who can deal with the beast."

Oh, so they got routed, huh? With that many people, they should have been able to win, but maybe the group got divided along the mountain trails. This was the first I'd heard of them losing, and noticing that, Albert smiled condescendingly.

"Don't tell me you haven't heard? I guess dealing with an owlbear is something far beyond someone with your skills, but the mountains are the pillar of your livelihood, right? You should really pay more attention to stuff like that. If you ask me, that sort of mindset is why you're an eternal D rank."

What was with him lecturing me out of nowhere? I just nodded perfunctorily as I glanced at Megria to move things along and get to the point.

"Sir, the time."

"Ah yes, time is of the essence."

The assembled party members nodded, too. It was really just a one-man crew centered around Albert. He was the only one with a noticeably high level. The rest didn't even meet B-rank standards. Other adventurers in the party rarely even spoke unless they had permission from Albert.

"Like I said before, we're headed out to take care of the owlbear, but we've hardly done any herb-gathering jobs. We don't really know much about the mountains."

"I see. So you wanted a guide?"

"Yes. We're more than capable of the actual hunt ourselves, of course. But I don't want to spend days chasing something like an owlbear. If we can get this done faster with you as a guide, then all the better."

"But I'm just a D rank, right? Wouldn't it be better to ask one of the adventurers in the first expedition that failed?" A look of contempt crossed Albert's face at my words.

"Huh? This is your chance, isn't it? All you have to do is guide us, and you'll get a nice accomplishment you can point to. You might even be able to get to C rank out of it. What are you so scared of?"

Judging from his annoyance, I could guess he had already been turned down. Most likely, the members of the previous party weren't sure Albert's group could actually beat the owlbear, or perhaps they feared that whoever acted as their guide might get caught in the crossfire.

It was rare for a B rank to be so distrusted in the face of something like an owlbear, but Albert was an adventurer who had come to Zoltan because he couldn't make it in Central. It was an open secret that the Zoltan Guild bent the rules a bit to recognize him as B rank because they needed one.

"Sorry, but I refuse, too."

"Why?! If you make it to C rank, you can take more jobs! And everyone else will respect you at least a little more! Even you don't enjoy being ridiculed, right?!"

"I've got no interest in being C rank. My dream is to open an apothecary and have a totally ordinary life."

"Kh, fine, then!" Albert shouted, glaring at me as he left in a huff. The rest of his party hurried after him. Left behind, Megria hung her head, embarrassed.

"It would be a relief if you were willing to accept this job. I can even guarantee the promotion to C rank, if you want."

"I'm sorry, but I really don't have any interest in that."

"Then there's no helping it, I guess. If you'll excuse me."

"Okay. Good luck." She bowed her head slightly and left to follow Albert's group. After watching her leave, I headed back into my house.

There was a thudding knock on the thin door as the sun was starting to set.

"Red! It's me! Gonz!"

"Oh, Gonz the carpenter? I'll be right out. Don't knock so hard. You'll break the door."

Judging from the sound of his voice, it was clear the woodworker was perturbed over something. I took just a second to slip my sword into my belt before opening the door.

"What is it?"

Standing on the other side was Gonz, the long-eared, half-elf carpenter. Despite still having the distinct, trademark elven good looks, he exemplified the hearty spirit and skill of a Zoltan carpenter. In a way, that unbalanced sort of appearance was fitting for a half-elf man.

"Sorry to bother you while you're resting, but my little sister's kiddo caught something. According to the doctor, it's apparently white-eye."

"Tanta got white-eye?! How far has it progressed?!"

"Ummm, as of now, he's collapsed with fever."

"The second stage of the sickness, then. Okay, I'll be right over!"

*   *   *

Since I was aiming to open an apothecary someday, I had been studying injuries, diseases, poisons, and various related topics. It had afforded me some familiarity with the afflictions. White-eye, as its name implied, was a disease where the corneas turned a cloudy white. It was a bird-borne disease. The pathogen attached to the eggs of birds, and eating an infected egg spread the disease to people. The disease could be killed off by heating the eggs, but it had some resistance to heat, so if the eggs weren't cooked enough, it would still be contagious. The reason the ailment was feared was because a few days after the initial symptoms emerged, the patient would go irreversibly blind. The first symptom was a high fever, at which point treatment had to be rendered within thirty-six hours.

Sight could be restored by Priest or Healer magic available to someone with a high enough level blessing, but…in Zoltan, on the frontier, there was only one person who fit that description. The previous mayor, Master Mistorm. She had retired in her old age, though, and was currently off somewhere enjoying her remaining years in peace. No one knew where she was now.

Gonz's little sister and her husband lived next door to the woodworker. Tanta was their son. The home was not particularly spacious but had a nice feel. It was furnished with a red roof and a weathervane on top and a green lawn with a small garden gnome out front. The whole design gave the building a rather cozy feel. It was a lovely home, built by Gonz and imbued with the love he held for his younger sister.

"Nao!"

"Gonz!"

His little sister, Nao, was also a half-elf, with fair white skin and a beautiful face. However, just like with Gonz, she had another aspect to her as well, the apron-wearing, child-rearing mother, born and raised on the blue-collar side of town.

Her husband, Mido, was human. He was a former adventurer who'd retired and now worked with his brother-in-law. Apparently, he was less adept at the work than Gonz, which led to a fair amount of scolding from the half-elf man, but Mido was quick at calculating and often covered for the rougher patches of Gonz's personality. When Mido wasn't around, Gonz would praise him for being a bright guy. If you asked me, it would probably be good to tell him that to his face once in a while, but evidently, Gonz couldn't bring himself to do that.

With their son developing white-eye, the couple's usual cheerful expressions had grown haggard.

"What do we do, Brother? There's no medicine..."

"It will be fine. We can trust Red. He's the adventurer who's gathered the most herbs in all of Zoltan."

That was where a normal adventurer would probably have lit into the man for saying such a thing, but to me, it was genuine praise. However, this was hardly the time to think about things like that.

"What's Tanta's condition?"

"The doctor's taking a look, but he said there wasn't anything else he could do without the medicine."

"Got it. Could you let me in?"

In the bedroom, there was the boy—Tanta—lying in bed, suffering from what looked like a particularly bad fever. The doctor, Newman, was at his side, observing his condition. He wore a serious expression.

"Doctor."

"Oh, so you're the adventurer Red? Thank you for coming."

"I heard it was white-eye."

"Yes, there's no mistaking it."

After that quick exchange, I examined Tanta's eyes, lymph nodes, and inside his mouth.

"Yes, his irises are paling, there are ulcers in his mouth, and the lymph nodes in his neck and underarms are swollen. He's got every initial symptom of white-eye, all right."

"I wouldn't have expected an adventurer to have such detailed knowledge," Newman said as he wiped the sweat from his brow and thinning hair with a towel.

"About how long has it been since he developed a fever?" I asked.

"Seems he was struck by a feeling of fatigue around noon, and he collapsed around three PM."

"It will be bad if we can't get him some medicine before tomorrow evening."

"That's the problem. I don't have any."

The medicine to treat white-eye was based on a preparation of koku leaves and a spiny mushroom called a blood needle. Excepting winter, koku leaves could be found basically anytime, but blood needles could only be gathered from spring into the middle of summer. Thankfully, it was spring, so they were in season.

"Last month, there was an outbreak of goblin fever and white-eye. None of the three clinics in town have enough medicine."

"I'm sure they have the koku leaves, though the blood needles... They're probably just starting to sprout, but..."

The Adventurers Guild managed the repository of medicinal herbs. Normally, they would be putting out job requests with a priority on gathering blood needles since the stock of those was running low, but...

"It takes time for that guild to approve anything."

Someone first had to point out that the reserves were low; the person in charge of those reserves then needed to report to their boss; the boss then double-checked the reserve; next, the person in charge had to write a report that their boss took to the higher-ups to get approval; and once that was all done, the person in charge had to fill out the forms to send out the job requests, which their boss had to double-check, and...

"Zoltan's Adventurers Guild is all about the red tape," Newman said with a grimace.

Anyway, right now, the fact of the matter was that there was no stock left of one of the fundamental ingredients for the medicine. Based on Tanta's symptoms, he needed treatment sometime before nightfall tomorrow. Considering that preparing the medicine from the ingredients took time, Newman probably needed to get the blood needles no later than noon tomorrow.

"I'm begging you, Red! I know the mountains are bad right now, but I've got no one else to turn to! Can you please get the ingredients? Name your price, and I'll pay! No matter how long it might take, I swear I'll pay it all back!" Gonz knelt, his head bowed to the floor as he pleaded.

"I mean it! The boy's a genius when it comes to carpentry! I can't accept his dream dying here like this!"

Gonz did not have any children. He lost his wife to sickness before I came to this town and continued to live alone, never showing any inclination of trying to find another wife. Because of that, he cherished his sister's son. So much so that he declared that the boy, who was not even ten yet, would succeed him in everything. Tanta was quite fond of Gonz, too. The boy was raised playing at Gonz's shop and was always saying that he wanted to be like his uncle when he grew up.

But...

"It's true that it's dangerous, but also the mountain is currently entirely off-limits. I might be an adventurer, but I can't go there until the owlbear is taken care of. If I ignore that order, I could get kicked out of the guild."

"Th-that's true, but there's nowhere else to get the medicine."

Nao and Mido both lined up beside Gonz, lowering their foreheads to the floor as they pressed their request.

...Albert and his party should've been searching the mountains for the owlbear by now. If they hadn't found it yet, they'd be camping out. It was also possible the party had found it and was busy tracking it across the mountain, even through the night. It was a big mountain, but they were experts when it came to hunting. Even the smallest trace could have given me away to Albert's group.

Should I negotiate with the guild? No, that'd be hopeless. I haven't earned that much trust from them.

"Big Bro, is that you?" Tanta's eyes had opened as he called out weakly.

The pointed ears proving his elven lineage were red to their tips from his fever. Yet the boy still smiled at me.

"Sorry, I caught a little cold. But once I'm better, let's talk through the plans some more," Tanta murmured. Gonz and the others glanced at me.

…It's not like the kid was saying anything of importance, though.

"Oh yeah. That promise to build my apothecary for me. Once you're better, we can talk about it some more."

It was just silly banter we shared when Tanta spent time with me. We talked about all sorts of stuff—like how I was going to build an apothecary, what sort of layout it should have, where it should be built, that sort of thing. The young half-elf had sworn to build it for me, saying "When I become a carpenter, I'll build your store for you, Big Bro Red."

Well, yeah. It was clear what I was going to do from the start. I mean, that was the promise, so there wasn't really any helping it. My beautiful, slow life wouldn't be complete without a modest but no less lovely little shop to go with it, after all.

"Right now, the Adventurers Guild has placed the mountain off-limits…"

"Y-you can't do it?"

"I can't take this job as an adventurer. But I'll do it as a friend. Promise you won't tell anyone?"

"Red!"

"I'll be back soon. I'll leave Tanta to you until then, Doctor."

"I'll do the best I can. But it will take an hour to prepare the medicine."

"It would take me three, so if you can do it in just an hour, I'd be grateful."

High-speed preparation was something that could only be done by people with a blessing in the Medical or Alchemical trees, or else maybe someone with the Herbalist blessing.

It was beyond my ability.

*   *   *

I had no intention of staying up in the mountains this time. I just filled a waterskin, secured my bronze sword, and left town. I jogged along the outskirts of the village a bit and then had a look around.

"All right, no one is watching." How long had it been since I last ran all out?

"High-Speed Mastery: Lightning Speed. Endurance Mastery: Immunity to Fatigue."

They might've been common skills, but by raising the skill level to 11, you gained access to the mastery ability. Quite powerful despite the skills being so common. Not many people built up common skills that high, though, so it wasn't a very well-known boon.

Lightning Speed increased movement by a factor of ten. While I was running, other people would see me as little more than a flitting shadow. Immunity to Fatigue meant my body wouldn't tire. Regardless of whether I was working through the night, engaging in heavy manual labor, or even sprinting all out for an entire day. Effects other than fatigue still applied; it wasn't as if I could go without sleep for days on end. Sleep itself was still necessary, but the skill was undoubtedly useful.

I took one powerful step, then another, and another. I gradually accelerated, and the scenery transformed into a green blur as I left it behind. Once I reached my top speed, I was covering one kilometer every thirty seconds, moving around 120 kilometers per hour. With magic support, I could run even faster, but this was my personal limit. That velocity could match the flight speed of an adult dragon more than one hundred years old.

As the last light of day was swallowed up by night, I sprinted toward the mountain. It took a while to reach my destination. If there had been even the barest of roads, I could've maintained my speed, but the rough forests of the mountain made moving that quickly unfeasible. I had to go normal speed here.

Taking out my map, I plotted my route.

I didn't want to take any longer than necessary, but I also wanted to avoid any route Albert's party was likely to take. I looked over the more common paths. This side got a lot of direct sunlight, and owlbears tended to dislike strong sun; hopefully, that meant it would avoid this area unless given a particular reason. Likewise, it would mean that Albert's party would naturally save this portion of the mountain for later in their search.

"All right." With a route set, all that was left was to move forward.

*   *   *

When I noticed the smell, I felt impatient for the first time in a long while and gritted my teeth as I ran.

"Dammit!"

The area where blood needles tended to grow in clusters had been scorched. My skill-enhanced hearing caught the shouts of Albert's party fighting in the distance.

"They used fire magic!"

Someone in Albert's party had used a fire magic while they were fighting the owlbear. Fire magic was powerful and the standard move when fighting something able to take a lot of damage, like an owlbear. But the conifer trees that blood needles grew on burned easily and were the perfect kindling for the hungry tongues of flames. On top of that, it was spring, when the winds were strong. It was incredibly dangerous to be summoning fire on the mountain, given the circumstances.

If it were Ruti or Ares, or anyone else from the party, they could have used an innate skill or a magic to extinguish the fire and halt the spread. But I couldn't do anything. I didn't have any means of extinguishing the growing blaze.

"Dammit! Dammit! Dammit!"

I used my bronze sword to cut the water bag I had brought with me and dumped it over my head. The only thing I could do in this situation was gather as many blood needles as possible. Goblin-fever season was over, but it was the time of year when white-eye, the deadly red-tongue disease, and the airborne trembling fever could break out. Blood needles were a crucial medicinal herb during Zoltan summers, and they were all being burned to ash.

Despite being so critical, blood needles grew in relatively few places. This mountain was the only major source in all of Zoltan.

I ran through the flames and smoke, plucking every one of the mushrooms I could find. The smoke coated my throat and scorched my lungs. Immunity to Fatigue did not help with smoke and oxygen deprivation, and the heat stung my flesh. But I could still move. I possessed no special skills. My blessing was a high level, pure and simple, and my resilience to physical punishment befit that level. I could take this much.

But there was a limit. Surrounded by flames, I started having trouble breathing, and hypoxia began setting in. The oxygen deprivation made my head heavy and dulled my senses.

A sudden rustling caught my attention. An owlbear covered in wounds stood before me.

You let it get away, Albert?

The wounded creature was in a frenzy. It raised its claws to attack, an instinctual drive to protect itself. I took the hilt of my bronze sword in hand. The wildfire had heated the grip, and there was a sizzling sound as it burned into my palm. The owlbear roared down on me, swinging its arms to tear me apart.

I drew my bronze sword, slicing upward across the owlbear's stomach to its shoulder.

*   *   *

"Over here, sir!"

Relying on the tracking ability of Campbell, a member of the party with a Thief blessing, Albert's party arrived at the owlbear corpse collapsed on the ground, its body encircled in flames. They had been granted Resistance to Heat and Resistance to Environment by a magic spell, so they were unhurt by the smoke or the heat of the blaze.

"That's a B rank for you! And I did my part, so I'll be getting my reward, too," shouted Dir the Fire Mage. He was hunched over, his cheeks were hollowed out, and his skin looked generally unhealthy.

He was the adventurer who had guided them in Red's stead, who Albert had only just barely been able to find in time.

According to Megria, he had a history of abandoning his party members and running away, rendering his reputation abysmal, but they had gone with him anyway, since no better option had presented itself. His poor guidance through the woods meant they'd been walking around the mountain until late into the night.

The owlbear wasn't moving, but Dir didn't dare draw any nearer to the beast. The creature would tear him apart if it was still alive, though it was a one-in-a-million chance.

Albert approached the owlbear and severed its foreleg. That would serve as the proof of having completed the job.

"We did it!"

"...This wound..."

"What is it?"

"No, it's nothing. Let's get out of here before the magic wears off."

Campbell the thief raised both his hands in agreement at that. "Yeah, even with the resistance magic, it's still hot and hard to breathe," he complained.

The woman with a Priest blessing furrowed her brow.

"That's just how it works. This isn't the sort of situation people were meant to survive in the first place. Just be grateful this is all the pain you have to suffer," she responded.

"I know, I know. Look, it for sure beats dying" came Campbell's response.

The effects of the magic that granted resistance to the fire lasted ten minutes. If it ran out while they were in the flames, even a B-rank party like them would be incapacitated almost immediately. The group of adventurers ran fast to escape the growing blaze.

✳   ✳   ✳

"Wh-whoa! Are you okay, Red?!"

It hadn't even been six hours since I left. By now, most folk would normally have been sleeping, but everyone was still awake and watching over Tanta. I rushed into the room as if I was about to collapse, my whole body covered in black soot.

"Dr. Newman, I got the blood needles."

"What?! That fast? How?! Wait…that looks like a really bad burn. What did you…?"

"This is all of the blood needles we're going to be able to gather in Zoltan this year… I'll explain later, but right now, preparing the medicine is more important."

"Okay, I understand. I'll get started at once." Newman took the bag of blood needles and went back to his clinic to get the medicine ready.

"Red, are you okay? I'll get something for those burns…"

"What's the point of going out to gather medicinal herbs if I have to take medicine when I get back? I'll be fine. The burns aren't as bad as they look. I'm going to go home to wash off. I'll be back soon."

"Wait! Red!"

I wasn't physically tired, but I could definitely feel that I had fully exerted myself. I poured the water from the well over the top of my head to cool my burned body. Looking out the window, I could see the crescent moon hanging in the night sky.

Even though I had gone all out, gathering a single bag of blood needles was the best I could accomplish. Such was the limit of my blessing.

Even pushing common skills to their limits, there was only so much I could do without innate skills.

"Guess it was only natural I got kicked out..."

If this was all I could do when I pushed myself to the max, then of course I wouldn't be any help saving the world.

*   *   *

At home, I gently washed the worst burns with a damp cloth and wrapped them in bandages before heading back to Nao's house.

"You three must be tired from nursing him the whole time, right? I'll switch with you and take care of wiping his sweat and getting him to drink water and all that until the doctor gets back," I said as I entered the room. But the three of them looked at me as if I were crazy.

"D-don't screw with me! You're the one who needs to rest!" Gonz shouted as he dragged me into the next room.

Some soup, a sandwich, and a bit of watered-down wine awaited me there. It had probably all been thrown together while I was washing off.

"Eat. My sister made it for you."

"Wait, taking care of Tanta's more important right now."

"We'll take care of him, so eat."

"Okay. In that case, I guess I'll accept this. Thank you." Sensing there wasn't any arguing with him, I sat down and started downing the food. Gonz was staring at me as I ate.

"What? Quit hovering; go be with your nephew."

"I never thought you'd get so beaten up."

"Albert's fight with the owlbear started a forest fire. I had to rush to gather as many blood needles as I could. I'm sure there will be more cases of white-eye, and it's a crucial ingredient for other medicines, too. It's a bit weird to say, but it was lucky Tanta caught it when he did. If he'd gotten sick tomorrow, all the blood needles would probably have been burned up."

"…Sorry. You ended up like that after doing so much to gather the medicine for us. Meanwhile, I was just sitting here on my ass."

"Don't worry about it. That's part of the job description for an adventurer. Besides…there's still the matter of my reward. You'd better steel your nerves."

"Y-yeah! A man always keeps his word! I'll pay up, even if it takes the rest of my life!" Gonz grinned broadly.

*   *   *

Thanks to the curative the doctor made, the cloudiness in Tanta's eyes cleared nearly immediately. It would still take a week of bed rest, and the boy would have to keep taking the medicine Newman had prescribed in order to completely heal, but there wouldn't be any lasting damage. With that, Newman declared that Tanta would be fine now and began packing his instruments back into his bag to leave.

"Thank you so much, Doctor!"

Gonz, Nao, and Mido lowered their heads, but Newman dismissed the action with a wave of his hand.

"It was fortunate he could get the medicine so quickly. With that, there shouldn't be any lasting visual impairment. It's all thanks to Red. And don't worry about my fee. Just put it toward covering his reward. These blood needles he provided are invaluable now, so I'll be discussing how best to use them with the doctors at the other clinics."

After hearing the news about the fire, Newman had grabbed both my hands and thanked me for gathering all the blood needles I had. He'd even offered to pay for the extras I had gathered beyond what Tanta needed, but I turned him down. Things that an adventurer gathered could only be sold to the guild. It was against the rules to sell directly to anyone else. Special permission was required in order to traffic items yourself. If I had sold Newman the blood needles, it would have been bootlegging, so it was safest to just give them to him instead of accepting any money.

"If I achieve my dream, I'm sure I'll be in your debt."

"An apothecary, huh? All the doctors in Zoltan would rejoice to have a skilled adventurer like you running an apothecary. Whenever you manage to open your business, please let me know. I'll be sure to patronize it."

"I'm looking forward to it."

Doctors were regular customers for an apothecary, so earning his gratitude here and making sure he remembered my name certainly didn't hurt.

Newman took my hand one more time and shook it firmly before returning to his own house. And after seeing him out, Gonz and his family bowed their heads to me.

"You really saved us. I can't thank you enough."

"Then shall we discuss my reward while the topic is still fresh?"

"Y-yeah! Don't hold back!"

"I don't plan to. In fact, I intend to get exactly what I want." The family looked nervous as I prepared to state my demands. When he heard it, Gonz was shocked but quickly broke into a full-faced grin.

I was sitting on a bench eating some sweet potato fries I had gotten from a stall as I watched the ceremony off in the distance. Tornado—the mayor—with his bushy beard on full display, stood on a stage and expressed his gratitude to Albert while awarding him the Twin Swords Medal.

With the battle against the demon lord's army heating up all across the land, these people were awarding the Twin Swords Medal for defeating a single owlbear. The medal was supposed to honor great deeds of combat. Here, it seemed more emblematic of how peaceful Zoltan was. The sight evoked a bit of a chuckle from me. All those gathered cheered and rejoiced when the medal was hung around Albert's neck.

"Tch, what's all the fuss over? He went and started a fire on the mountain."

"Oh, Gonz? Didn't you say you weren't going to take today off, even though you're always first in line for festivals? What're you doing here?"

"Who'd take a day off to celebrate him, knucklehead? I'm just here to get some lunch." Gonz was holding a basket with a sandwich, some fried food, and a few other assorted bits. He sat down next to me and took a fried fish out of the basket and started eating.

"If you ask me, you're way more deserving and amazing than he is."

"Oh? Then let me have that." I grabbed one of the sausages out of his basket and bit into it. Gonz looked angry for a second before breaking into a hearty laugh. We sat there for a little bit watching Albert's ceremony.

"Albert's doing his best for the town in his own way."

"Hmm? He is?"

The B-rank adventurer still had a Central-esque air about him. Often, it didn't leave a good impression on a lot of people from the blue-collar parts of town. People like Gonz. The stuffy, formal clothes made of multiple layers that were popular in the capital were considered too hot and irritating to the people in Zoltan. However, the mayor and what few well-to-do folk who lived in the town did cling to an appreciation for a more Central sort of style. So Albert was well received by them. It was possible the man was even intentionally maintaining those trappings simply to earn favor with the wealthier denizens of Zoltan.

"Well, it might also just be that he hasn't gotten used to life on the frontier."

"What are you talking about?"

"Albert. Don't be too harsh on him. He drifted in from Central and is doing his part as a B-rank adventurer in a party that struggled to deal with an owlbear. I'm sure he's got a lot of pressure he's dealing with every day."

"That so?"

"And even so, he's trying to make it work. It's not like he wanted to burn the mountain down."

"If you're okay with it, then I guess I'll leave it be," Gonz said, resigned. His tone made it clear he still wasn't convinced. He obviously thought I should've been the one getting the accolades. But I just wanted to live a modest life; I didn't really need them.

I watched until Albert left the stage, and then I patted Gonz's shoulder and said good-bye. Starting tomorrow, I was going back to gathering herbs. Also, I had reported the mountain fire to the guild, but the extent of the damage still needed to be assessed.

If I was going to run an apothecary, I needed to get a handle on the best remaining places to gather medicinal herbs before anyone else. I was serious about trying to make my dream a reality here in Zoltan.

※   ※   ※

"That wound..."

After the ceremony and the meal with all the influential people in town, when Albert was finally alone, the B-rank adventurer thought back to the image of the owlbear collapsed on the ground.

"That wasn't damage I inflicted... My sword wouldn't make that kind of cut."

It was a slash all the way up the torso to the shoulders. Rough, the cut looked like it had been made by a dull weapon that had been forced through with incredible power.

"Like...a bronze sword."

The image of the D ranker who the man had tried to get to guide his party flashed through Albert's mind. He'd...had a bronze sword on his waist, hadn't he?

"There's no way."

Albert shook his head. "Besides, there's no way he could have been there," he muttered to himself.

※   ※   ※

Four months and two days later. According to the calendar, fall was right around the corner, but in Zoltan, there was no end in sight to the heat of summer. The town still displayed vibrant greens, as if it had no interest at all in the fall styles adorning the mountain and other regions. The area that had been burned in the fire was already covered in plants again. The black scar of burnt foliage was no longer visible.

I made my way to a part of town a bit outside the town center. It was in the area between a residential neighborhood and a district where craftsmen plied their crafts. It was a ten-minute walk from the residential block where my town house was. At a normal person's walking speed, of course.

"You finally made it, huh?" Gonz said.

"You're so slow, Big Bro Red!" Tanta shouted.

The two of them were wearing neat, formal suits and waving their hands. I had slipped myself into a rented suit for the first time in a while, too. In the past, I'd been made to deal with aristocrats and royalty with my sister fairly often, so it wasn't my first encounter with a suit. This was the first time since I'd left the party, though.

Behind Gonz and Tanta stood a newly constructed building. It wasn't that big, but its design spoke of strong, solid construction. Visually, it had a reassuring sort of feel. There was a sign above the front entrance that read:

Red's Apothecary.

This was the reward I had asked Gonz for. Money for the materials came from my own pocket, but the construction was free. The savings I had built up at that point were enough to cover the construction thanks to that arrangement. Today was the gathering to celebrate the successful completion of the build.

I looked up at the sign, overcome with emotion.

"Everyone's waiting to eat, so hurry it up already!" Tanta said, grabbing my hand and dragging me in.

"All right, all right," I answered as I was led inside.

Around twenty people, ranging from Gonz's coworkers, some

members of the Adventurers Guild, Dr. Newman, and a few others with whom I got on well in Zoltan, were all gathered in waiting.

"Oh, the man of the hour's finally here."

"You've really gotten used to Zoltan's pace, Red."

I had been busy sorting out various medicines for the store's opening and had lost track of time. In Central, the star of an event being late would have caused an uproar, but here, it was forgotten with a laugh. I scratched my head as I thanked everyone who had assembled, and then we started the banquet.

"Mom made the food for today!" Tanta announced, oozing with pride.

He was almost as proud of his mother's food as if he had made it himself. When I commented that it was delicious, he happily fired back immediately with "Right?" and a delighted smile.

There had been no further complications to Tanta's white-eye. His eyes were sparkling like a young boy's should, and he was laughing just as cheerfully as he did when working with Gonz or his father.

Newman made a point of thanking me again and saying how fortunate it was that we were able to get Tanta the medicine so early in the disease's progression.

"I'm pretty sure I already sent you the order. If you've had a chance to look at it, do you think you'll be able to fill it?"

"Yes, it won't be a problem. I'll put a priority on the delivery and get it to you tomorrow evening."

Dr. Newman was my first customer and had promised to place requests for whatever herbs he was running low on periodically. He'd even given me a recommendation when I was registering my shop with the Merchants Guild and let me know that if I borrowed the funds for opening the business from them, they would put the paid interest owed on the loan toward my first year's guild membership fee. Despite not having to pay construction costs, I'd run my savings nearly completely dry just purchasing the materials, so that sort of recommendation was particularly helpful. Now I wouldn't have to worry about losing my operating rights for failing to pay the membership fee.

Not bad for my first step.

"Oy, don't you have any big aspirations or anything?" Gonz asked.

Aspirations, huh…? It was hard to answer such an out-of-the-blue question… But everyone was watching me; I wasn't in a position just to say nothing.

"Ahhh, yeah…"

I tried to compose myself and think of a suitable answer but quickly thought better of it. I wasn't going to try to put on airs like that. I wasn't a knight or a member of the Hero's party anymore.

"With all your help, I've managed to realize my dream. Thank you. But now I'm going to try to take it easy while running this apothecary and not push myself too hard. Particularly on hot days like today, I just want to sit back, drink some cool tea, and chat with everyone. So feel free to come by to hang out anytime."

The room erupted in laughter and applause.

And just like that, I started my slow life as an apothecary in Zoltan.

▶ ▼ ▼ ◀ ◀

Chapter 2

- - - - - - - - -

Tbe Priŋcess Who Didŋ't Joiŋ tbe Hero's Party

▶ ▲ ▲ ◀ ◀

Reports that the Hero, Ruti, had defeated the second of the four heavenly kings—Gandor of the Wind—and captured the sky palace over which he claimed dominion had made it all the way to Zoltan. Gandor boasted countless wyverns at his command and wielded an aerial battle strength said to have been the strongest in the world. It was thought that a minimum of five times the number of the villain's own forces were required just to contend with his army. Even the demon lord's army would be on their back foot with the setback of Gandor's defeat.

"Ruti's really giving it her all."

On the Zoltan frontier, the menace of the demon lord's army was still like something happening in a far-off world. The people of Zoltan cheered the victories that the continent's united forces won, but rather than a sense of the menace receding, it was more like a festive sort of celebration.

A chime brought my thoughts back to the world around me. It was the bell on the door.

"Welcome… Oh, Gonz and Tanta?"

"Yeah, we came by to play. I see it's as empty as ever in here."

"Don't start in on it."

It was rainy outside. Carpentry jobs were put on hold during such weather. With the temperature during the day breaking ninety-eight degrees, almost all of Zoltan was generally pretty laid-back this time of year.

Adventurers didn't really want to work much in this sort of heat, especially when a downpour could start so suddenly. There were many who saved up during the winter and spring and took a break during the summer. But goblins and other creatures that pillaged and plundered didn't take a break. Summer heat did little to cull monsters that attacked people, either, so higher-ranked adventurers with a sense of responsibility, like Albert, were constantly running around dealing with them. I'd been busy gathering stuff for my shop, so I hadn't done much work as an adventurer as of late. My more pressing concern was what to do about the lack of customers coming to my shop.

"It's only been half a month since you opened, and you've already had some decent sales, haven't you?"

"Thanks to some introductions from Dr. Newman. I'm wholesaling medicinal herbs to the other clinics, too, but…"

"'But if normal customers don't come,' right? Well, this time of year, everyone's just lazing around their house, so they probably can't work up the energy to walk all the way down to the apothecary."

"After I went through the trouble of stocking up on the medicine for summer colds…"

Medicines had an expiration date. After a few months, I would have to get rid of all the stuff I had prepared and all the herbs I had gathered, too. Before, the Adventurers Guild would only pay less than a fifth of the medicine's retail price, but at least they would buy all of it and take it off my hands. Compared to that, I was sitting here anxiously waiting for anything at all.

"Well, you'll get more customers as time goes on," Gonz said with a hearty laugh, but this was hardly the time for joking. "Speaking of, have you eaten anything, Red?"

"No, I haven't yet."

"All right, let's go get some food."

"Nah, I'm trying to cut back on eating out. I've been making my own meals here."

"Huh? You can cook, Big Bro?" asked Gonz's nephew.

"I sure can. You can't be an adventurer if you can't cook."

After all, food is essential. On a painful and harsh journey, food might often be the only highlight. For me personally, bad food was so painful that I put a few points into my Cooking skill, even though I knew it wouldn't be of any use at all from a combat perspective.

At first, Ares was vehemently against it, but Ruti and the others gave the cooking high marks, and after a few days, Ares stopped complaining. In fact, he even started shamelessly asking for seconds. Meals were some of the few times when my comrades relied on me, even though I held them back in nearly everything else.

"Ohhh, you don't say."

"Well, obviously I can't win against someone with an actual Chef's blessing, but it's pretty decent for an amateur. Want to give it a try?"

"Really?!"

"Sure, just wait a bit."

The shop had also become my new home. The floor plan included the storefront and storage area, as well as a bedroom, kitchen, washroom, living room, and a work area for preparing medicines. There was also a modest yard out back for growing my own herbs.

Thinking back on it, it was actually pretty big. Was what I paid for the lumber and materials really enough to cover it all? Gonz might have gone a bit overboard for me.

I opened the shelf in the storage room where I kept my food and thought a bit about what to make.

"Potato salad, bacon and eggs, and tomato soup. Something along those lines?"

Putting the food into a basket, I headed to the kitchen.

*   *   *

"Here you go; order up." I set the food on the table in my living room.

"Ohhh, I wasn't sure what to expect, but this looks pretty good," Gonz said.

"I'm not a cook, so all I can make is basic home-style food."

I may have set the bar a bit too high. I was just trying to say it was pretty good for an amateur, not that I had some particularly great skills when it came to cooking... Well, it was too late to change anything now.

"All right, don't mind if I do."

There was chilled water with a bit of lemon floating in it to drink. I had also prepared some herbal tea for after the meal. The lemon and herbs were both things I had picked up while gathering medicinal herbs, one of the little perks of the job.

Tanta took the bacon and eggs, Gonz, the potato salad, and they both grabbed a spoon and took a bite.

"How is it?"

"...Wait, really...?"

Gonz and Tanta both froze.

"Wh-what? Do you not like the taste?"

"No...this is seriously delicious."

"This is amazing, Big Bro! This is even better than Mom's cooking!"

The two of them stopped talking and quietly dug in to their plates. I relaxed a bit and started in on the soup. Yep, it was pretty delicious, if I did say so myself. Once they'd finished, the two sipped at their herbal tea with satisfied looks.

"But why was it so delicious? The food itself wasn't anything that special."

"Hmm? Yeah, maybe because the seasoning was good?"

"The seasoning?"

There was a lot more growing on the mountain than just herbs for making medicines and antidotes. From the base to around halfway to the peak, the mountain's temperature went from a tropical climate to a temperate one. As you got nearer to the peak, it became subarctic. There were classic, well-known spices like mustard, garlic, cinnamon, and nutmeg that all grew in abundance on a single mountain. Even some lesser-known plants grew fairly plentifully. So if you just used the seasonings the mountain provided when preparing the food, it would taste good...probably.

"Huh, I never would have figured you'd know so much about cooking."

"You can only do really simple cooking on the road, so I don't know anything when it comes to elaborate dishes and special ingredients, though."

"That's more than enough. With food this good, you could open your own restaurant."

"You're not getting more than the tea, no matter how much you flatter me."

"The tea's delicious, too."

The herbs for the tea were also ones I'd collected on the mountain. My guess was that the wood elves who had lived in Zoltan in the past had selectively bred them, and then, over time, the plants they had bred came to grow wild on the mountain. On this continent, there were a lot of fruits, vegetables, and domesticated animals that had been bred from wild species by the wood elves over a very long period.

The country of the wood elves had been destroyed in the great war with the demon lord long ago. Their blood now survived only in the veins of half-elves mixed with human lineages. Half-elves like Gonz and Tanta were descendants of those wood elves.

But even if the wood elves themselves hadn't survived, the knowledge of natural science they had built had been passed on to humans. What I knew of medicinal herbs and medicine, I learned from a wood elf book.

A bell chimed from the storefront.

"A customer? I'll be right back. Make yourselves at home."

"All right."

A customer coming in from the rain was rare. I hurried to the front of the store.

"Welco—"

A young woman in an odd outfit had entered. She was wearing a full-length black robe with a hood, and she was covering her mouth with a blue bandanna that was wrapped around her neck. The flowing hair peeking out from her hood was golden. The hilts of two large, curved swords—shotels—with griffon feather ornamentation were visible at her waist.

Every resident of Zoltan knew this girl. She was the other B-rank adventurer, though her true strength far exceeded Albert's. She always worked solo, never teaming up with anyone else, and despite that, she still rated equivalent to a B-rank party. With her abilities and a proper party, she'd easily make A rank. Possibly even higher. Her name was Rizlet, though everyone around these parts called her Rit. Apparently, she'd chosen not to use the name Rizlet here in Zoltan, choosing specifically to go by a pseudonym.

Rit lowered her hood when she saw me. Her sky-blue eyes were fixed on me.

"…So you really are here, Gideon."

My expression tensed. *So she's finally come.*

Her real name was Rizlet of Loggervia. The second princess of the Duchy of Loggervia. For a short time, she had been part of my old party, one of our comrades. She was also known by the second name of Rit the hero. That was the name registered with the Adventurers Guild in Loggervia, and it was also the one she used in Zoltan.

I had Gonz and Tanta leave. They were surprised to see the strongest adventurer in Zoltan and were pretty suspicious about what sort of connection we had, but they accepted it when I explained that she had come by for a consultation about some curatives.

Once they'd left, the two of us sat across from each other at the living room table. Steaming cups of tea rested in front of us, untouched.

"Um, I… Well, here, I'm called Red."

"Yes, it seems like that's what you've been going by."

In Loggervia, despite being the second princess, Rizlet would often sneak out of the castle and fight in the colosseum under the name Rit. She even took part in battles against the demon lord's army as a mercenary. We met her during our journey. The first time we met, she'd made a point of her hostility toward us. Later, we saved her from some trouble she'd gotten into. Afterward, we escaped a siege and adventured together to call for reinforcements. It seemed like she was often pretty back and forth on whether to join our party at that point. In the end, we went our separate ways. She had stayed behind to help tend to the wounds the battles had left on her nation.

It always felt like, if we'd said slightly different things at the time, she would have joined Ruti's party.

"I was a little too conspicuous, and voices from certain corners started calling for me to succeed Father and become queen over my younger brother, the crown prince. Before it devolved into a family feud, I ran away to the frontier to play around a bit until things settled down."

She and Albert took care of the highest difficulty quests in Zoltan. While Albert tended to prioritize jobs from influential people and avoid ones he felt weren't worth his time, Rit took the initiative on the most difficult quests, making her more popular among the general public.

But that made sense. Given her reasons for coming to Zoltan, being an adventurer was basically just a hobby. She took the more difficult quests because they were more interesting. The girl had plenty of funds available because of her family, so money wasn't an issue...

"Which reminds me, the name Red... Rit. Red. They have a similar sort of ring to them."

"Yeah, about that... The truth is, I couldn't really think of a name, so I sort of based it off yours." I glanced at Rit's red clothes.

When I was thinking up an alias to use as an adventurer, the image of the adventurer who had left the strongest impression on me in the past—Rit—was what came to mind. That was also part of why I ended up choosing the name Red. That part was embarrassing, though, so I wasn't going to say it out loud.

"…Hmm, so you were using me as a reference."

"Sorry I ended up with a name that could so easily get mixed up with yours. I can't really change it at this point, but I hope you can forgive me."

"…I'm happy about it!"

"Huh?"

Rit lifted the bandanna around her neck, covering her mouth as she grinned. Oh yeah, that reminds me, even when we first met, she had this strange habit of covering her mouth whenever she smiled. It always made me suspect she was from some upper-class family. Not that I would have ever guessed she was a princess, though.

"Because you remembered me."

"Well, yeah. Even if it was just for a short while, we were comrades! There's no way I wouldn't remember you."

On top of that, something as unprecedented as a militarily inclined princess would obviously leave an impression.

"Comrades… That you would still call me that…" Rit glanced down a bit and fell silent.

Right. When we'd parted ways back then, Rit had said we were the first party she could call true comrades. The first group she'd teamed up with had left Rit behind and run away when faced with a scissor-hands demon, a powerful monster. At the time, we were also after that creature, and we ran into her and worked together to defeat it. After that, you'd think Rit's attitude would have lightened up a bit…but it didn't. She got easily embarrassed and ended up unnecessarily butting heads with us even more to hide it.

Ruti found it annoying, but I enjoyed talking with Rit when she kept getting into it with us like a cute little puppy, so I kept her company fairly often.

"So, Gide—no, it's Red here, right…? What are you doing here?"

"About that…"

I honestly would've rather not explained that I was kicked out of the party because I was useless…but there was no way she would accept any other explanation. Plus, I needed to make sure she didn't tell anyone about me.

I guess there was no helping it.

"It's a bit embarrassing..." I steeled my resolve and told her the story.

* * *

"What the hell?!"

After I finished, Rit snapped for some reason. "After you fought together for so long?! That's crazy!"

"Even so, it's not like there wasn't some logic to what Ares said. It was certainly true that I was a hindrance."

"There's no way that was true! You were the one always paying attention on how to keep the party moving smoothly!"

That was true. Since I recognized my lacking battle strength, I did pay attention to various other things in order to be helpful in areas outside combat. The cooking was part of that, as was monitoring the condition of the rest of the party, gathering information about new towns, acquiring whatever consumables we needed, managing the finances, negotiating with various influential people who wanted a meeting with the Hero...

"See? You were working superhard!"

"When you actually list it all, yeah, I suppose so."

Rit still didn't seem willing to accept reality. In fact, she looked about ready to explode.

"You don't need to get so angry. I probably would have ended up getting defeated somewhere down the line because I couldn't keep up with the flow of battle. In fact, it's probably just as well that I retired to Zoltan and started my apothecary before that happened."

"Wait, with you doing all of that for them, are they really going to be okay without you now?"

"I'm sure they're fine. Apparently, they even defeated the heavenly king of wind not too long ago."

Or at least, that was the news that made it out here. But this far away from the front lines, reports went through lots of people and were basically just hearsay on arrival. Them actually defeating Gandor was almost certainly true, but all the specifics had likely been exaggerated.

I'd be lying if I said I wasn't a little bit worried, but...

"Even if I worry, there's not much I can do now that I've left. Ruti was always traveling with me, so I'm sure she can make it work somehow."

I couldn't deny that part of the reason I was saying that was to try to convince myself. But I wasn't in Ruti's party anymore. As her older brother, there wasn't anything more I could do for my precious little sister.

"That's enough of this topic. Whatever points we might make, it's not like Ares is here to listen to them," I said, trying to placate Rit.

"Ugh... I guess so," she responded, still clearly not ready to accept what I already had. I happened to glance down and noticed the cups I had placed on the table.

"The tea got cold. I'll make a bit more."

"It's fine. You don't have to do that for me."

"It's not every day we get to meet back up again. I want you to be able to have some proper tea, not like before where I had to throw together whatever was available."

In the past, when I was making something, it was because we were camping out in the wild or stationed on the front lines. All I managed back then was whatever could be thrown together from the supplies we carried or what could be gathered on the road. It was never anything made under optimal conditions.

Things were different now, though. I had my pick of the plants growing on the mountain. I could find tea leaves as good as anything sold in the markets and use naturally clean water instead of water that had been purified using magic. The purified stuff always had a sort of inorganic flavor to it.

I quickly took the cups, cutting Rit off, and headed to the kitchen to make some more tea.

I raised the temperature on the pot of water sitting over the flames until finally it started to steam. My personal theory was that the temperature right before it started to boil was best suited for the tea leaves I had. I watched the pot closely, careful not to miss it, waiting as the water quietly swirled.

Suddenly, I recalled making hot milk for Ruti when we were both still children. We didn't have sugar, but I added some honey that I'd gathered from the forest and had her drink it. Ruti always hated drinking milk, but she'd looked shocked when she tasted it with honey, then glanced at me before drinking half of it in one gulp. Once she realized that only half was left, she started sipping at it bit by bit. She'd sighed happily when it was all gone.

Having been born with the blessing of the Hero, Ruti always seemed to have a farsighted point of view, but I still remembered how cute she was drinking milk like a normal child.

"There we go."

I took the pot off the flames and added the tea leaves. A nice fragrance started filling the air, and I nodded to myself a little.

"It's delicious…"

Rit let out a satisfied exhale. It was entirely different from the ones Ruti made when she was a kid, but it still gave me a small amount of secret satisfaction.

"Back then, I was shocked that the Hero's party was eating such delicious food while out camping, but with proper ingredients, this might even be better than the tea in the royal court."

"That's a bit much, even for flattery. My Cooking skill is just level one. I've got some ability compensation from my level, I'm sure, but I can't beat a proper chef."

"Still…" Rit lifted the cup to her lips and took another sip. "…Maybe it's so delicious because you made it just for me." The girl whispered the last part softly, her cheeks flushing a bit as she smiled.

Rit had never been that honest back when we first met.

✳   ✳   ✳

The first time I met Rit was in her homeland, the Duchy of Loggervia, in a town called Alomar, near the southern border. We had come to the duchy because we'd received reports that they were struggling to deal with the demon lord's army's offensive there. Loggervia was in an important location strategically, which meant if they fell, several neighboring countries would be toppled as well. It needed to be protected no matter what.

At the time, the party consisted of Ruti the Hero, Ares the Sage, Danan the Martial Artist, Theodora the Crusader, and me, the Guide. The five of us were at a tavern eating as we mulled over information we had managed to gather around town. It was around when Ares was talking about a reported sighting of an orc spy from the demon lord's army.

"Hey, missy, let's share a drink."

We heard the catcall of a rough voice. Glancing at the counter, I saw a woman wearing a black hooded robe and a hunchbacked man with a dangerous leer in his eyes calling to her. His cheeks were extremely hollowed out, and his skin looked deathly pale. A lead club wrapped in several layers of leather hung at his waist. It was a weapon called a sap, designed to knock out an opponent without killing them. It was often used by slave hunters, a trade I had cracked down on more than a few times when I was still a knight. I'd never carried a good impression of those who used such weapons, and my tenure as a knight did nothing to change that view.

"Hey, don't ignore me. Name's Dir. I'm actually a pretty well-known mercenary in Sunland, you know. You've heard of Dir before, right?

You haven't? Whatever. Let's just have a drink. Come on." He peeked at her face beneath the hood.

"Whew, aren't you a cutie," he said with a whistle.

You could find guys like him in any town you went to. Ruti and I stood up, about to move in to stop him, but...

"Owwwwwwww?!"

The robed woman grabbed the hand he had put on her shoulder and twisted it upward, knocking the ruffian back as she stood up.

"Wh-what are you doing?!"

She lowered her hood. Her blond hair fluttered gently, and her clear-blue eyes shone with a strong will. A small, indomitable smile crossed her lips as she looked down at the man who had been knocked on his ass.

"Y-you!"

He started to rise, his right hand forming a sign in order to activate a spell.

"A Fireball?"

A fire magic spell that caused an explosive blaze. It was not something to be using inside a building, even in a fit of anger. I hurried to try to stop him, but before he could activate his spell, the girl in the black cloak drew a sword with an arched blade—a shotel—decorated with griffon feathers and held it to his neck.

"You picked the wrong person to hit on."

"S-sorry! Pardon me!"

Seemingly sobering up, the man's face grew a shade of alabaster as he trembled and ran away.

I guess we didn't need to worry about it.

Relived, Ruti and I started to go back to our seats, but the robed woman turned her determined gaze toward us.

"Did you think I needed your help?"

"We were worried over nothing, it seems," I said with a forced smile.

She stuck her finger to point at Ruti instead of me, though.

"That's right! We don't need the Hero here. We can take care of the

demon lord's army ourselves in Loggervia!" proclaimed the girl with a self-satisfied grin. That was the first time I met Rit—Rizlet.

$$*\qquad\qquad*\qquad\qquad*$$

With her chest all puffed up, Rit explained that the royal guard of Loggervia was well trained and that the people living up in the mountains provided the country with a wealth of lumber. With that lumber to burn for fuel, the government could forge high-quality weapons and armor to provide to even the lowest-level soldiers, so there was no way the Duchy of Loggervia would lose to the demon lord's army. Having said her piece, the girl made a prompt exit.

"It seems like she was just waiting for us to come here."

Well-connected informants should've already heard news that the Hero was on her way to Loggervia. If we were going stay someplace, then Alomar was the logical choice, and if we wanted to gather information, then that would be the center of the town. Which would mean this tavern was the best spot. The girl had likely thought along the same lines and guessed right.

"..." Ruti looked dissatisfied, and I smiled at her when I saw her expression.

"It's been a while since we got that sort of a reception. Don't forget how hard you worked before we left the capital, before anyone believed you were the Hero."

"I know." Ruti still seemed annoyed as we returned to the table.

$$*\qquad\qquad*\qquad\qquad*$$

"I give up! I give!"

He was the last of eleven thugs. Holding his swollen face, the man cast aside the club he was using as a weapon.

"Sheesh."

The thugs had been paid one payril each by the man who'd been shown up by the girl in the bar. Apparently, they were planning to lie in wait to attack the black-robed young woman. I happened to catch word of it while gathering my own intel, so I decided to take care of them myself.

"A-are you with her?"

"No. I haven't even had a proper conversation with her. I just saw her in the tavern. Even if I didn't help out, though, I doubt she'd have had any trouble with you."

"Is she really that strong?"

"I only caught a glance, so I can't say for sure. Do you know any black-robed, blond-haired shotel users?"

"Wh—? Isn't that Rit the hero?" The thugs started muttering among themselves. Some of them even seemed relieved that I had stopped them.

"Rit the hero? Is she famous?"

"You're not from around here, are you? Of course she is! In Logger-via, Rit's crazy famous. She's the strongest A-rank adventurer... Screw a measly silver; I wouldn't take the job even if you offered a thousand."

"Her party is A rank, but word is she's the one doing all the work."

"She's even the champ in the arena here. She can't be beat when she goes up against a humanoid opponent—a real league of her own."

It's not as if they were acquaintances or anything, but the thugs seemed almost proud of this so-called Rit the hero. That much was clear from their tone.

"I see. Well, in that case, I guess you've got no more intention of trying to do anything to her."

"Of course not. Even if we tried, we'd be the ones who'd end up getting hurt."

They didn't seem to be lying. They'd already been generally roughed up, and it wasn't as if they had even done anything yet.

"Got it; then you can go now."

I waved my hand, and they happily said their thanks and made themselves scarce. They started sharing their stories about Rit's feats with one another as they dragged themselves away, battered and bruised. I almost laughed to myself over their childlike reaction.

The next day, one of the thugs I had beaten up told me that the guy from the tavern had thought they were still going ahead with the plan. He'd ambushed Rit by himself and got beaten half to death before being run out of town. The thug seemed veritably happy as he told me the story.

"Man... Rit the hero is crazy awesome, isn't she?"

He sounded almost proud of her.

Several days later, Rit showed up at the lodge where we were staying. She didn't do anything, though, just ordered some food and sat there eating quietly. Seemed like she was in a bad mood.

From time to time, she would glare at me and mumble, as if about to say something, but in the end, she left without a word.

✳   ✳   ✳

"Back then, you were really standoffish. No matter how many times we fought together, you were always complaining about something."

"B-but what about that time we were investigating that mountain village? I was more honest about how I felt then."

"Huh?" Thinking back, I tilted my head. That was honest?

It was when our party and Rit's party were sort of competing— investigating a disturbance in a village up in the mountains. It was a small settlement of lumberjacks, and the firewood they provided was used to fuel the workshops of Loggervia. The reason the duchy was known as a military powerhouse was because of the excellent weapons and armor those workshops produced. The gear was then provided to even the lowest-ranking soldiers.

A sudden disruption in that fuel supply line occurred, and the adventurers and knights who had been sent to investigate didn't return. That was how we ended up looking into it. That was also where Rit's party intervened, with her saying that they would take care of it themselves.

"So no progress today, either?" The black-robed girl—Rit—called out to me.

I was sitting on a log in the village's small plaza, snacking on some dried fruits and cookies.

"A late, lonely lunch for three days straight, huh?" Rit observed with a smirk.

It was three in the afternoon, definitely late for lunch. She sat down on a log opposite me.

"For being the Hero's party, you guys aren't so hot when it comes to gathering information, huh?"

"It is what it is."

It was certainly true that Ruti was not particularly great at intel. When it came to that task in particular, there were plenty of other blessings better suited for the job. For example, Rit's Spirit Scout blessing had useful skills for tracking footprints or finding even the most minimal traces of something's presence. Compared to her, our group was far more focused on combat abilities. When it came to scouting, we made do with Ares's and Theodora's magic and my experience as a knight to get by, but it was not an area in which we specialized.

Our goal was to fight the demon lord's army. Slipping into the enemy's camp alone and defeating their commander was a daily sort of feat for us.

"Ha-ha. Our investigation is making pretty good progress," Rit said proudly.

"Uh-huh."

"Do you want to know?"

"Yeah, you mind telling me?"

"All right, if you ask nicely and say 'Please, Miss Rit, could you please tell a fool like me?' Then I'll tell you."

"Please, Miss Rit, could you please tell a fool such as me?" I asked immediately.

"Huh?" Her smirk disappeared when she heard that.

"My pride's a cheap price to pay for being able to save Loggervia. I'd gladly say it as many times as you want."

"Wh-what—? That wasn't what I meant... Sorry."

"Oh?"

This time, it was my turn to grin. Rit's face turned red as she glared at me.

"What's with that look all of a sudden?"

"Nothing, nothing. Just surprised you were actually able to honestly apologize."

"Y-you! Fine, I won't tell you, then!"

"I'm sorry. So what have you managed to learn?"

She seemed to have gotten annoyed, looking away from me and holding back for a bit before finally heaving an unnatural sigh.

"I guess it can't be helped," she said, starting to share details.

"I had a look around the vicinity of the village, and there were footprints coming and going with a high frequency recently in the north."

"The north, huh? There was a lodge out there for logging, if I recall."

"But right now, the logging is going on in the northeast. I even went to check to be sure."

"And you've got the other two in your party watching things there at the moment, right?"

"You knew that?"

"Even if I'm not a great investigator, I can at least perceive the basic movements of people."

"Hmph. So do you know why I have the two of them waiting there?"

"Because even though the supply of lumber going out has stalled, logging is still happening."

"What's with that 'I already know everything' face? You're no fun at all." Rit glared at me, looking a little disappointed.

"I'll take that as a compliment. So have you figured out where the lumber is disappearing to?"

"We've only been watching for three days. It hasn't been long enough to say yet."

"Were there no traces of the timbers being carried elsewhere?" Rit's face clouded over at the question.

"That's... I still haven't found any."

"So magic, then."

"Probably."

There was no way something as big as felled trees could be carried away without leaving traces that someone as good as Rit could find. Which meant it was safe to say the culprit was using magic to float them through the air, or perhaps shrink them small enough to fit in a bag, or transport them via some kind of portal.

"Why do you think the villagers have said nothing about it?" Rit asked.

"Hostages, probably. There are too few older people and children in town. I saw toys and empty cradles and stuff like that in many of the houses."

Noticing that no one was around, I had checked out the homes in the village over the past three days. I couldn't find anyone hiding but was left with the impression that the current population didn't match what one might expect given the homes. The children and elders had been kidnapped, and the rest of the townsfolk had been frightened into obedience in exchange for the safe return of their loved ones.

The rest of my comrades were spread out searching for the location of the captives, and I was in charge of checking out the village myself, which is why I was here eating lunch alone.

"Which means it's a group organized enough to manage hostages," Rit concluded.

"That would mean it's not a local group of thieves or goblins," I responded.

"Not a surprise."

To confirm that we had reached the same conclusion, we both said it at the same time:

""The demon lord's army.""

Exactly as expected. No surprise there, either. But if the demon lord's army was involved, then the mastermind would be powerful.

"Hey, Rit, maybe we should work together on this one."

"Huh? Me, work with you? Quit dreaming!" she shouted as she stood up and pointed her finger at me. "We can beat the likes of the demon lord's army, no problem, even without you guys lending a hand. They've already attacked twice before, and we sent them packing both times. Loggervia doesn't need some outsider hero!"

"But the groups that attacked before weren't the main forces. Those were orc units. There will be soldier demon tercios and a detachment of Gandor of the Wind's wyvern knights, too. The commander is an Asura demon, the same race as Taraxon, the Demon Lord."

"What of it?" Rit just sniffed disdainfully. "From the day it was formed, the Duchy of Loggervia has never lost territory. Not when the goblin king, Mulgarga, went on a rampage fifty years ago and not during the Lightning Dragon War seventy years ago, either. Loggervia has never lost. This time won't be any different. We'll fight. We'll win. That's all there is to it."

"But fifty years ago, your great uncle asked for help from Central. Loggervia's pride isn't so petty as to fail to do the things necessary to increase the chance of victory, right?"

Rit was at a loss for words. Her eyes trembled for a brief moment.

"Why do you know about our history?"

"How could we ask someone to fight with us without knowing anything about them? Your ancestor was truly an outstanding hero. There weren't many countries able to make it through that goblin mess unscathed."

Rit's cheeks flushed. She covered her mouth with the bandanna around her neck. But her expression soon took a serious bent, and she looked at me with a gaze backed by an iron will.

"It looks like you've at least done a little bit of homework... But no. I'm going to resolve this myself. If I do, Father won't have to do something like give command of part of the royal guard to the Hero."

"...I see."

So that was why Rit was so adamant. Rit's master was named Gaius, the head of the royal guard. Rit respected him greatly. Rit's father, the ruler of Loggervia, had proposed shifting a portion of Gaius's command to us. That was something that Rit could not accept. She'd always possessed a sort of independent streak to sneak out of the castle on her own, and she was trying to prove that Loggervia could fight on its own, that they didn't need help from the Hero.

But from our perspective, command of an actual force, particularly the Loggervia army's strongest royal guard—even if it was just a small part of it—would be a big deal. More than a few times in the past, we had been left wishing and wondering what could have been if we had the strength of such a force at our command.

Both Rit and my own party had our own reasons for trying to resolve the circumstances afflicting this village.

"In that case, I guess there's nothing to be done," I said.

No matter what I said, Rit wasn't going to back down here. All we could do was just let her get to know us better in the course of resolving this and during the fight with the demon lord's army to come.

"Do you have any guesses about where in the north they're hiding?" I asked as I spread out a map. Rit sighed and then sat down next to me and peered at the large chart. I handed her the bag of the cookies I was eating and a pouch of water.

"What?"

"You're on limited rations, too, right?"

The reason I was eating preserved food that I had brought with me, despite staying in a village, was because I was on guard against being poisoned. With hostages having been taken, there was no telling what the villagers might do. We were staying in the village chief's house but had found dehydrated poison hemlock in the kitchen, though he'd assured us it was just for exterminating rats.

Even if we chose to overlook the fact that they were trying to poison us, and even if they were doing it on orders, that didn't change that they'd attempted the deed. And Rit was Rizlet, the royal princess of Loggervia. Regardless of coercion, the mere attempt would be grounds for a death sentence. So both Rit's party and ours had turned down the food offered to us from the first day on, choosing to get by on our own rations. From what I could see, her party was only eating salted meat and pickled vegetables. It was definitely the kind of thing you would get sick of after a few days.

"If it tastes bad, I'm going to be angry," she said as she took a hard-baked cookie and bit into it.

"Mm..."

"How was it?" I didn't miss that she broke into a smile for a split second.

"I-it was okay."

Seeing her struggle to keep up appearances, I couldn't help but grin. Rit was indignant, but that didn't stop her from reaching out to grab another.

"Where do they sell these? They aren't Loggervian."

"Yeah, I made them."

"Huh? You did? The cookies?" Rit looked back and forth between my face and the food, in shock. "Why?"

"It gets old eating salt-preserved rations every day. A little bit of cooking is a fundamental requirement for a long journey."

Biting into the second cookie, Rit contemplated what I'd said for a moment.

"Yeah, you're right about that." She nodded in agreement.

"See? I can be honest," Rit insisted, pointing out that last bit.

"Really?" Laughing along at the memory, I couldn't help expressing my firm disbelief that Rit had really been honest there.

The girl ended up joining in the laughter, maybe from recalling how she had been back then.

"Do you remember what you said after we finally found the scissor-hands demon hiding at the base in the north and fought it together?"

"...No..."

"I believe it was, and I quote: 'Not too shabby...but don't get the wrong idea. I've only very slightly revised my opinion of you! Just a little, so don't get full of yourself!'"

Rit buried her face in her hands and lay across the table.

"Uggggh, I was just trying to do my best in a lot of different ways back then, okay?" Apparently, dredging up that memory of the stand-offishness she fell back on to hide her embarrassment was mortifying because even her ears turned red.

The point where she really did become honest had been during the decisive battle with the commander of the demon lord's forces in Loggervia. The confrontation with the Asura demon, Shisandan. The outcome of that battle was not exactly a happy one, though...

✳   ✳   ✳

Rit and the Loggervian adventurers were supposed to be attacking the rear of the enemy's camp.

The camp was that of the approaching contingent of the demon lord's army. The force was under the command of Shisandan, a fiend from the same tribe as Taraxon, the Demon Lord. Shisandan was a six-armed Asura demon.

Shisandan's invasion consisted of not just orcs but heavy infantry demons and wyvern knights. Such a force was powerful enough that even the elite soldiers of Loggervia could not hope to challenge them. Several of the duchy's fortresses, villages, and settlements had already been taken. The country was on its way to downfall. If they couldn't win the coming fight, there would be no future for Loggervia.

The head of the royal guard, Gaius, the man who had taught Rit swordsmanship, had taken his forces to act as a diversion. Meanwhile, Rit, who had been sneaking out of the castle and making a name for herself as an adventurer, returned to the castle that was on the verge of falling. With her, we worked to defend it.

Using the fame she had gained as Rit the hero, she successfully rallied the troops to her, and they were able to hold the western gate that had nearly fallen. Despite such accomplishments, most of the knights had rejected the blond girl's proposed plan to launch a sneak attack, deeming it too dangerous.

Only one person, Gaius, supported her plan and swore to deploy his own troops to draw attention away from her movements. Unfortunately, the truth was that the actual Gaius had already been killed. Shisandan had used magic to assume his appearance. The royal guard were elite forces, but with their commander being the enemy in disguise, they were caught off guard by the demon lord's troops and hastily massacred.

Rit had intended to spring a sneak attack where the enemy least expected one, from behind. Instead, her force was met by a fully prepared enemy and in a position where they were sure to be wiped out.

"Where's Gaius...? What did you do to Master?!"

"I ate him, since I needed his memories, 'my favorite student,'" Shisandan had said in the voice of the princess's beloved teacher.

Rit roared and leaped at the fiend, but she was quickly overwhelmed by the countless demons and pushed down to the ground.

"I'd wager that if I took your form, the hero hailed by all the people of this land, it would be even easier to capture this country. What do you think?" Shisandan, still wearing Gaius's face, spoke with a sinister joy.

Rit found herself in tears. A person she'd truly held dear was dead, and now countless more would suffer because of her failure.

At that point, there was a whistling sound of something cutting through the air. The next instant, my sword was sticking out of Shisandan's shoulder.

"Wait, Gideon! You're too early!"

I could hear Ares complaining. It would've been another twenty seconds before my comrades finished reaching their positions surrounding the enemy. Because I was the fastest of the group, I had gone ahead to check on the situation by myself. Unable to sit by and watch, I had leaped into the fray before everyone else had time to prepare.

For the next few moments, things were chaos. I knew the monstrous forces of the demon lord would try to protect Shisandan. Without the party's help, slaying the fiend was going to be difficult, but...

"There's no way I'm abandoning Rit! She's one of us!" I shouted as I cut down the demons restraining her.

My sword had been the trusted sword of a ghost knight who protected an underground tomb. It was a treasured weapon said to call forth lightning when it was swung. The unsheathed blade of Thunderwaker flashed in the evening sun, and the demons recoiled in fear, like children cowering at silver lightning crackling through the sky.

We'd pursued Rit after discovering the truth about Gaius at the last second.

"Gideon..."

"Don't cry, Rit! If you're one of us, then face the enemy with your swords drawn, not tears!"

"R-right!" Rit wiped away her tears with a muddy sleeve and replaced her frightful look with a warrior's resolve. The girl picked up her blade that had fallen to the ground.

"Ruti and the others won't take more than a minute to break through from the outside. Until then, we have to stop the Asura demon and keep him from escaping. Can you do that?"

"I can!"

"Then let's do it!"

We charged at Shisandan, whose false human face wore a confused expression.

"The Hero?!" Shisandan shouted, seeing Ruti running toward us.

My sister hadn't reached us yet, but the mere presence of the Hero's martial prowess was enough to dull Shisandan's blade. Rit and I fought back-to-back, bellowing battle cries at the countless demons charging at us from every direction as we swung our swords.

When you meet a close friend for the first time in a long while, the day seems to fly by. The rain had stopped long before we ever took notice, and the sun was getting pretty close to the horizon. Soon it would be time for the sky to turn red and the town to be shrouded in the dark of evening. But even so, we sat at the table, reminiscing about old times.

There was finally a moment when we both were silent. At that point, Rit's eyes wavered briefly before she finally spoke.

"Hey, Red."

"What, Rit?"

The young woman was looking straight into my eyes.

"Can I work here, too?"

"Huh?" I couldn't stop the dumbfounded exclamation. I definitely hadn't expected that.

"Red & Rit's Apothecary has a nice ring to it, don't you think?"

"W-wait a minute. You're one of only two B-rank adventurers in Zoltan."

"I'll retire."

"Wait, wait, wait!"

Did she hear what she was saying? Wanting to work at a shop with no customers from noon till night?

"As you can see, I only just opened up shop, and it isn't exactly thriving. I don't really have the cash flow to hire staff."

"But when you go out to gather more medicinal herbs, who will watch the store for you? Isn't it a waste to close up shop while you're away?"

"Ugh. Well, that's true, but I mean, what customers?"

"That's because you only just started. You'll get more in time. Why don't you show me around?" Unwilling to wait for an answer, Rit stood up and walked around.

"Hmm?"

"One counter and a display case on either side. Uh-huh. Pretty straightforward."

"Because I only have the standard sorts of herbs and medicines on display. The ones with more limited quantities or that need special handling or storage are kept in the storehouse, or else are growing in the backyard."

"There's plenty of room to work here. With this much space, you could have an assistant helping."

"I don't have any plans to hire anyone for a while, but we'd probably work pretty well together."

"And then a kitchen, a washroom, a bedroom, and the living room we were chatting in before. You've got yourself a nice little store."

"I know, right?"

Rit started nodding as she mumbled something to herself. Listening closer, it sounded like some kind of calculation.

"Considering Zoltan's economic situation and your skill, you're looking at probably around one hundred and eighty payril a month after expenses, maintenance, and taxes."

"What?! ...That's all?"

I could earn around a hundred just gathering herbs for two days and selling it to the Adventurers Guild, but doing the same thing for my own shop was only going to net me 180 a month?

"Really? I'm doing the gathering myself, so I don't have to pay for raw materials."

"Medicinal herbs aren't the sort of thing that have particularly high consumption rates. Unlike the guild, which wholesales to apothecaries, you're selling to customers and doctors. It will take time for you to sell out what you gather. You could probably get by with just one excursion a month."

"Gngh."

That was all I could sell? But medicinal herbs could be used in so many ways.

"First of all, you may have forgotten, since you became a knight so early and then were part of the Hero's party, but an average person's expenses are only around thirty payril a month."

"Yeah, I knew that, but..."

"A normal apothecary making one hundred and fifty payril a month would be thriving. That hundred and eighty is based on the assumption that the people nearby get to know you and that you'll be able to actually grow your business."

The herbs that the Adventurers Guild bought from me were sold to apothecaries and traveling merchants at a higher price. I had thought I could make more money selling them directly myself, but thinking it through again, the reason the Adventurers Guild could always sell at any time was because of how good their market connections were. Even if an independent shop had a stockpile of medicine, it would take time to unload it all. I had been thinking that I could just make things work if I could sell what I'd gathered and made myself in my own shop, though that might have been a bit naive.

"But yeah, thirty payril is enough to live on."

Like Rit said, I had become a knight at a young age and had a pretty solid series of promotions all the way up to second-in-command of the Bahamut Knights. Back then, my living expenses were around three thousand payril a month. It was a lifestyle along the lines of an aristocrat. The place I lived was a residence on the grounds of the palace, and I even had a maid to help take care of everyday necessities.

When I was traveling with Ruti, we got tens of thousands of payril from the spoils of fighting the demon lord's army and recovering treasure from dungeons, and we traded that for expensive miracle potions and weapons made from rare ores. I was pretty numb to how much normal people had to spend.

"Huh... Anyway, you're pretty knowledgeable on the subject."

"I was still a princess, you know, even if I ended up like this. I studied a lot of things back at the palace. And when I went out, I worked at several different stores as a bodyguard. I would usually make small talk with the owner about how their business ran." The girl puffed out her chest a bit as she bragged. It reminded me of how she had acted when we first met. The thought brought an unconscious smile to my face.

"Also, it would probably be good if you had a medicine or something that no one else had... But since you don't have an Herbalist blessing, finding a recipe is..."

"I've probably got something unique to fit the bill there, if that's what you're wondering."

"Eh? You do?"

Actually, developing recipes for medicine had nothing to do with skills. Recipes were just a simple question of knowledge. Skills didn't get into the mix except at the actual preparation stage. Even if you found a useful recipe, if you didn't have the skill to mix it, you wouldn't actually be able to complete the medicine. So realistically, it was standard for people without an Alchemist or Herbalist blessing to develop a new recipe.

Since I never had any innate skills, I was always groping around for anything I could do. During the journey with my old party, I had the opportunity to learn from documents and the knowledge of both the past and the modern era. Even stuff left by wood elves and the ancient elves who were destroyed in antiquity. In terms of pure knowledge regarding preparation, I doubt I'd lose to an actual alchemist. Though it would be a pain to explain it all if I ever brought that up to anyone, so I never bothered.

"If I recall, they're in storage."

Rit and I headed over to the storage room.

"These two are original medicines of mine that I can make in Zoltan."

I pulled out an ashen-gray potion in a cheap-looking bottle and a pill small enough to fit on the tip of my pinkie.

"What do they do?"

"This one is called the multiplying potion."

"M-multiplying potion?"

"Yeah. If you take a preexisting magic potion and dilute it down to one-fifth using this, you can make five of the original."

Magic potions did not have the effect of medicinal herbs. They were potions made by sealing away magic. White berries were often used as catalysts for magic potions. The white berries themselves didn't have a special effect on human bodies, but by using the liquid extracted from them and various other things depending on the magic you wanted to bottle, it was possible to seal it away.

By drinking the magic potion, the magic would activate, and you would achieve the same result as if the magic had been cast. However, the magic potion had to be consumed in order to have any effect, so generally speaking, healing and support magics were the ones usually made into potions. Attack magics could be made into potions, but they wouldn't do anything unless you could somehow get your target to drink them.

But magic potions were extremely expensive. A cure potion based on level-1 recovery magic that could be found in any town cost fifty payril, so it was used as an emergency medicine for normal people and the lowest-level mercenaries, just for when they were in danger of dying. For C-rank and higher adventurers, they might gulp it down as they took on a powerful enemy.

"The ingredients for the multiplying potion cost about five payril. If I was going to put it on the market, then…I guess I'd probably go for around four times that, so twenty payril. If you think of it as being able to make four copies of a seven-hundred-and-fifty-payril Extra Cure potion, then…I think it will probably find a market…um…but…" Rit turned over the contents of the potion bottle in her hand.

What was the problem? I thought it was pretty revolutionary. And when we were traveling, we used it to increase the number of Extra Cure and Magic Power potions we had. Even Ares didn't have any complaints.

"…You can't sell this."

"Really? …What's wrong with it?" My shoulders slumped. I really had some confidence in that one. I couldn't believe Rit didn't think it was good enough.

"What's wrong?! If you sold this, it would totally depress the market for magic potions! It would effectively cut the cost of every potion by eighty percent!"

"B-but I figured it would be okay, since it can only create more of an already existing potion. You'd still need the original first."

"The very existence of this potion would be a huge problem… If you sold this, the Adventurers Guild, the Mages Guild, the holy church, and probably even the Thieves Guild would come after you."

I started to laugh, but it looked like Rit wasn't joking.

"This is just potions we're talking about, right? Not some magic item that costs more than ten thousand payril."

"Those magic items are custom made one-offs. The majority of sales, the thing that drives actual economic activity, is the relatively cheap potions that everyone can use." Rit was staring at me with a troubled look, but after a second, her eyes softened.

"Pu-ha-ha...ah-ha-ha-ha-ha!" Suddenly, the blond girl burst out laughing and started slapping my back. I was dumbfounded, with no clue at all what was happening.

"Sorry, I just got this feeling of super-relief."

"Relief?"

"I had this image of you as this amazing person. Always coolheaded, able to do all sorts of things, able to keep calm even when charging at the demon lord's army in the midst of a fearsome battle... And even when I thought everything was hopeless, you appeared like a flash of lightning to save me... You always seemed so untouchable."

"I'm not that great."

"No, Red, you really are that great. If you actually took all the steps and went through the right process and released this out into the world, lots of people would be saved, and it would help a lot in the fight with the demon lord's army. But what I didn't realize until just now was that there are also things you don't know—and things you don't notice."

I wasn't sure what was so funny about it, but she was practically in tears. I would never have guessed she thought so highly of me. By the time I met her, I was already starting to fall behind the rest of the party in battle strength. Ares and Danan had gotten really mad at me for running ahead when I saved her from Shisandan.

"So is the illusion broken?"

"Nothing like that. It just made me think that I wanted to be with you a little more," Rit said as she stopped laughing and lifted her bandanna with a finger, covering her mouth as she glanced away. Her ears turned a pinkish-red shade.

"Um, yeah, it seems like I'd probably have trouble running this place by myself." I looked away from her, too, struggling to get the words out as I rubbed the back of my head.

Yeah, I should have just acknowledged it. I didn't dislike her affection. In fact, I was surprised by how happy it made me. I was sure it was because Rit was one of my comrades from back when I was known as Gideon. That she would still acknowledge me even though I had been declared a hindrance and pushed out of the Hero's party… It let me think that maybe the journey I had struggled so desperately to keep up on, where I had been nothing more than baggage, hadn't been entirely for nothing.

"I can't promise much for pay…and you don't have to work here all the time. Just come by when you feel like it… But I'd like it if you'd help me out."

"Sure! You don't have to add the bit about when I have free time, though, since I'll always be with you!" This time, Rit didn't hide her mouth with the bandanna, instead smiling broadly.

Excited, I started to head back to the living room, but there was still one medicine I hadn't explained.

"Ah, um, this pill is something I made after coming to Zoltan."

"Don't tell me it has the same effect as an Extra Cure potion or something crazy like that."

"That's impossible. It's a new kind of anesthetic."

"Anesthetic?"

"The effect isn't any different from the one currently used, but it is less likely to cause dependence."

The current anesthesia used for surgical procedures was very addictive, so there were a lot of people who became dependent on it and even overdosed well after they actually needed the drug. Medical treatment without anesthesia was so painful, though, that even adventurers struggled to endure it. There was also the possibility of going into shock and dying from the pain and loss of blood. So despite the risks, anesthesia was still indispensable.

"The less addictive, the better, right? It was a medicine I found in the journal of an adventurer who traveled across the dark continent, but the ingredients all grow here in Zoltan, too. They might have been brought over and cultivated by wood elves. Either way, though, it's a new anesthetic. Normal people won't need it, but doctors and adventurers might be interested. What do you think?"

"Yeah, that should probably be fine. It will likely be a nice source of income... But you should get approval from the Zoltan council first."

"The council?"

"Even if it is less addictive, it is still an anesthetic. I'm sure some people will start wondering whether it could be used as a narcotic. Getting approval first means you won't get an order to stop selling it later."

"That makes sense."

"There's no telling how a new drug like that will sell. If the demand for anesthetic usage in town comes to us, that would be a pretty good source of income. If that happens, though, we might not be able to keep up with demand."

"All it needs is the common skill Elementary Preparation. We can produce even more if we take on another employee."

Rit froze when I said that.

"Right, you're so amazing that I forgot about it for a second, but this only takes Elementary Preparation to make."

Pretty much all effective anesthetics required the skill Intermediate Preparation. In that sense, this medicine suited me well. However...

"The medicine itself is great, but it might be a problem that someone without a relevant blessing can make it..."

"R-really?"

"No one in town knows about your blessing, right? As long as we sell this in normal amounts, we can probably just pass it off as you having a blessing that has access to Intermediate Preparation."

"Hmm, an Herbalist with the advanced skill Preparation Analysis might be able to reverse engineer the recipe by analyzing the medicine, though," I added.

"You really have a wealth of knowledge when it comes to blessings.

Normally, no one would know the innate advanced skills for a random uncommon blessing."

Knowing someone's blessing meant knowing the tricks they might have up their sleeve. With a few notable exceptions, it was the same for monsters, too. There were plenty of race-specific blessings, but for the most part, monsters had the same blessings as humans. In the monster realm, Warrior, Barbarian, Thief, Sorcerer, and Adept were particularly common, so if you knew as much as you could about those five, then you could generally anticipate how the enemy would fight.

Particularly in my case, since I didn't have any skills of my own to rely on, I used that knowledge to fill in the gaps. For example, I realized early on that Rit's blessing was Spirit Scout. A blessing with access to spirit magic as a hidden trump card. When it got harder for me to contribute in battle, there was a period where I would charge in first in order to get a grasp of the opponent's abilities, so I could tell the rest of the party ways of dealing with them.

But that only lasted until we started facing more and more Asura demons, the race that formed the bulk of the demon lord's army. They were the exception rather than the rule. Asura demons were the one and only beings in the world that lacked Divine Blessings. Even animals had them, but not Asura demons. Some referred to the fiends as God's failed creations. However, in exchange for not having blessings, it was said that Asura demons could fuse together to gain new abilities. I can't say whether that part was true, but it was true that Asura demons had a system of skills that was a mystery to me.

"There shouldn't be any herbalists in Zoltan with access to advanced skills. So as long as you limit the sales to Zoltan, you should be fine. If we only produce as much as you can make by yourself, then there shouldn't be much getting into the hands of traveling merchants, either."

"Good. Then if any customers ask, I can say that I have a blessing with access to Intermediate Preparation."

"Please do. It might risk raising questions about why you haven't stocked any medicine that requires Intermediate Preparation, though. So only mention it if someone asks."

"I'm not going to go out of my way to tell a lie."

Truth was always preferable to the alternative. If you didn't lie, then you never had to worry about being caught. "Silence is golden," as the Ancient Hero supposedly said.

"The Ancient Hero, huh?" Rit said, moved.

The story of the Hero of old who fought the demon lord back when wood elves ruled the continent was treated almost as a fairy tale. Lots of people doubted the veracity of it, but with the appearance of Ruti, a modern-day Hero, the existence of the Hero Divine Blessing had been proven, so scholars were reevaluating their stances on the Ancient Hero, too.

Currently, archeologists and bards were apparently investigating ancient town records and murals in cities long abandoned, searching for records and stories of the Ancient Hero.

"It's got nothing to do with me now, though."

Right, I reminded myself. I wasn't involved in that stuff anymore.

✻   ✻   ✻

Apparently, we were talking for a while in the storage room. By the time we realized it, the sun had almost set, and the red sky was about to give way to darkness.

"Want to have something to eat?"

"Yes, please!"

That much excitement was enough to make the cook in me happy, so I decided to put a little extra effort into the meal. I headed to the kitchen, considering what to make.

"I haven't had a chance to go shopping yet, though. If I'm throwing something together with what I've got, then…"

Chicken leg cut into chunks and boiled in water with grated ginger. Once the chicken was soft, I added two halves of a potato and a boiled egg. Once the potato got soft, I added some pasta, salt, and herbs for seasoning… It was done before I knew it.

Southern-style pasta soup. During my travels, throwing out the water that had been used to boil pasta was a waste, so I ended up making a lot of pasta soups. This was a recipe I'd picked up during those experiences. I hoped Rit would like it. A twinge of nervousness gripped me as I brought out our bowls.

*   *   *

"It's delicious!"

"I'm glad you like it."

Rit was sitting at the table with her bandanna, usually around her neck, set aside as she deliciously chowed down on my cooking. It really was great having someone enjoy your cooking.

"And I'll get to have your cooking every day now."

"Hmm? I guess so."

Apparently, she was planning on coming by to eat every day. Well, preparing food for friends was one of the small pleasures in life for me; I was fine with it.

"When do you normally eat in the morning?"

"Hmm? Ah, usually around half past seven or so?"

"In that case, I'm going to have to actually make a point of getting up a bit early. Working as an adventurer, I always end up staying in bed when I don't have anything going on. I'll have to do my best to fix that!"

Evidently, she also intended to come by for breakfast, too. Was she planning to eat all three meals here? I couldn't really afford to pay her that much, so covering some of the salary with food was probably fair.

Starting tomorrow, meals were likely going to get very interesting.

"Oh yeah. I'll cover the cost, but we should get a proper bath made, too."

"A bath? I mean I'd be glad to have one, but you don't have to go that far for me."

"It's fine, it's fine. I'm going to be using it, too, after all."

…She apparently intended to bathe here, too… Wait…

"There's only the one single bed. We're going to have to buy another one tomorrow."

"Yeah. H-huh?"

"I'll bring whatever personal stuff I need over, but I can just leave the furniture in my old place."

It seemed an awful lot for a job. It's almost like she was…

"Ha-ha, it's almost like you want to live in my house."

"Ha-ha, I mean, yeah, obviously, since I'm moving in."

"Eh?"

"Eh?"

Wait a minute. When did this turn into her moving into my house? The building was decently sized since it also had my store, but the living area itself wasn't that big.

"I said it before, didn't I? I'm going to quit being an adventurer and work here."

"Oh yeah, you did sa—? Wait, what? How does that lead to moving in here?"

"Since I'm quitting adventuring and working here, it would be more convenient if I was also living here, right?"

"I—I see. I guess that makes sense… If you say so."

"I do say so."

"Okay."

"Okay"? Well, to sum up it basically meant that Rit was going to be living with me from then on.

"…Uh…huh? Wait a minute, wait a minute. Isn't that kind of bad?"

"Why?"

"I mean, if we're living together, then, like…"

"What's the problem? We slept in the same tent before, right? There'll be even more space between us now than there was then."

"But that's just because when you're camping out, there are only so many tents. We just naturally ended up having to share a tent."

"Isn't it the same? We're comrades, aren't we?"

"Mn? Uh? I mean, yeah, we are."

"Then it's fine for us to sleep together in the same room."

"Really?"

"Really."

Was it, though?

"All right, I'm going to go clean up, so I'll be using the washroom."

"S-sure. Do you have a change of clothes?"

"I always just throw stuff into my item box."

"I mean, that helps, but should you really just be doing that?"

"There's a comfy little yard here, so if there's some time, I can just hang my clothes out to dry in the sun."

"Hmm, then do you want some help with that?"

"It's fine, it's fine... But if you don't mind...?"

"Sure."

...Wait, were we going to sleep in the same room?

There was only one bed, but still...

Chapter 3

Let's Start Our Slow Life Together

The next day.

When I opened my eyes, I was a little confused to feel the hard floor beneath me and realize I was wrapped in a cramped sleeping bag.

"...Oh yeah."

Seeing Rit's face as she lay asleep on the bed, I remembered our back-and-forth last night with a pained chuckle. When it came time to sleep, we got into it about who would get the bed.

Rit offered to sleep on the floor, of course, but I insisted on her taking the bed. After a little arguing, we nearly both ended up sleeping on the cold planks but settled on deciding it with rock-paper-scissors. I won in the end, which meant I was the one who had to forgo sleeping in the bed.

"What a silly argument."

Since we were both well acquainted with sleeping outdoors, it wasn't like a night in a sleeping bag was a big deal. Thinking about it now, there wouldn't have been any problem if I had taken the bed, either.

"Well, what's done is done. Guess I should make some breakfast."

Zoltan summers were sweltering even in the morning. In the rest of the world, it was already autumn, but here there was still another month of summer left. Outside, cicadas were buzzing away. Part of me despised the noise while another part appreciated the summer sort of feel they provided. I crawled out of the sleeping bag and headed to the kitchen.

"Ugh, hot water?"

The water I was storing in the pitcher hadn't cooled at all overnight.

"Ahhh, lazing around the house on days like this is the Zoltan way."

But drinking hot water wouldn't stop the sweat. It was a nuisance, but I decided to fetch some water from the well.

✳   ✳   ✳

I was carrying four jugs filled to the brim that were hanging off the end of a pole. Generally speaking, here in Zoltan, water taken from the river was for routine daily uses, and water taken from the well was for drinking. Most people had a preference for mixing some diluted wine or ale with the water to drink. Even children drank it that way, despite the alcohol content.

"Heave-ho… Things would probably be a bit different if more people out here had blessings with access to magic, though."

I set the vases in a dark corner of the kitchen. With as hot as it was, if I put them someplace where the sun might shine on them, they'd likely heat up pretty quickly. Maybe even hot enough to boil an egg.

"Speaking of eggs… Bacon and omelets? And lettuce salad and potato soup. Oh yeah, I didn't go get bread yesterday. I've got some flour, so I could make crepes to wrap around the salad and omelets."

Once I settled on what to make, all that was left was to do it.

As I busied myself fixing breakfast, Rit's smile while she ate dinner the previous night crossed my mind. It was only the first morning since she had moved in, but it felt as if she had already become a regular part of my life.

✳   ✳   ✳

"Morning," Rit said groggily.

"Got up early, eh? Good morning."

Even without me going to get her, she'd managed to wake up herself around when I finished cooking. Seeing me, she flashed a smile and headed to the washroom to clean her face.

"I've got some cold water in the kitchen you can use if you want."

The water supply in Zoltan got tepid in the heat of summer, but Rit just shook her head with a smile.

"I'll be fine."

I heard her cast some magic from the washroom. She had used a spell to cool the water.

"Must be nice…"

Thinking of the effort it took to go the well in the morning and draw water, it made me jealous of blessings with access to magic. While she was getting ready, I set the food on the table.

"Wow. It looks great."

Rit returned from the washroom. Despite the fact that she had just cleaned her face, she still looked a little out of it as she sat in the chair. Her voice was still slightly groggy, and her pajamas were a bit disheveled. A shoulder peeked out from the wide and awkward resting place of the top's collar.

"Not much of a morning person?"

"Yeah. Since it was a new bed, I didn't sleep quite as well as I usually do."

"Are you really that sensitive?" I asked.

"Hmph. Thanks for the food." She declined to answer my question as she started to eat.

Despite saying she hadn't slept well, Rit still looked kind of satisfied, so the trouble sleeping probably wasn't because my bed was cheap. I just smiled a bit and grabbed my spoon. We avoided small talk as time slowly passed during the late-summer morning. The blond girl poured some of the cold water with lemon floating in it into her cup and glugged it down.

"It's delicious." Rit happily enjoyed her breakfast to a tune sung by a choir of cicadas. Her verdict on the meal made me smile.

*　　　　*　　　　*

Once we finished eating and cleaned up the dishes, we had some cool tea while discussing what to do today.

"Do you want to clear out your item box to dry like we talked about last night?"

"No, we should do the other stuff first. We can take care of that anytime."

"Okay, then shall we get your bed and whatever personal effects you need?"

"No, my bed wouldn't fit in that room."

"...You've been enjoying a nice bed, huh? I guess that would explain having trouble getting to sleep."

"That isn't why I couldn't fall asleep. I'm going to get a new bed, but I also planned on bringing a few paintings and things that would suit the store."

"Paintings?"

"You shouldn't discount how much impact artwork can have. The right kind of piece in a good spot can definitely help increase sales."

"Ahhhh."

I guess that was true. Shops with a nice atmosphere did sort of just draw you in.

"Should we stop by to get some kind of gift to go along with the application for approval from the council to sell the anesthetic while we're shopping?" I asked.

"Sure."

It wasn't as if there was some kind of official requirement that you had to give the bureaucrat a gift when you made your request. In fact, there definitely wasn't. However, it was rare for a country to have strict rules and procedures when it came to making decisions like that. And this was Zoltan, famous for being an idyllic, easygoing sort of place. The official in charge of medicines was the person who would decide whether a new drug received approval or not. A lot could change depending on his impression.

"We're a newly established apothecary, so it might be better to go for one on the more expensive side, since the store itself hasn't built up a good reputation yet."

"I know. I'm pretty experienced in these kinds of negotiations."

Actually, running a store was a completely new to me. However, during my adventures, I had been the one who dealt with the influential people wherever we ended up going.

Something along the lines of a gift valued at thirty payril should've been just fine. Things made of a precious metal that could be resold for close to market value were generally preferred. Something like a piece of silver tableware was pretty standard.

"That reminds me, not just the gift, but we should get you a dining set, too."

"You don't need to do that. I'm fine with using your stuff."

"I've got a pretty decent set, but I never anticipated needing more than one person's worth. It's just a numbers problem."

"If that's all, then fine. I'll cover it, since it's my share."

"I'd rather you not get anything expensive, so I'll pay for it."

I was used to a pretty cheap living, so dealing with expensive tableware for everyday stuff all of a sudden would be scary. Feel free to laugh at me for being a coward if you want. If I was holding a plate that cost half a year's income, I would end up being overly careful with it, which would take up time I needed for other things.

"It's not like you have to treat it particularly carefully just because it's expensive. A set of tableware is expendable."

"Even so."

Back in my old party, I had also managed all the finances, so I tended to be a bit tightfisted when it came to money.

"All right, then I'll take you up on your offer, I guess. While we're on that, though, about my salary."

"…Yeah," I responded with a gulp.

Rit wasn't the type to demand some outrageous amount, so that at least wouldn't be a problem, but…

"What do you think of one and a half payril per day, for a total of thirty per month? I'm getting room and board, too, so I think that should be pretty reasonable."

It was a little on the low end for a store employee, but like she said, it was perfectly reasonable when considering the room and board. But Rit was a B-rank adventurer. There's no way she wasn't raking in at least ten thousand payril in that line of work. Considering her means, thirty payril was pretty lacking.

"Got it. Then we'll go with that."

It would have been a lot worse if she'd insisted on not taking any payment. If Rit refused compensation, I wouldn't have been able to accept it and would have offered her a salary. That's just the kind of person I was. The amount definitely would've been higher than thirty a month, too. Her proposed salary, which was pretty in-line with the market rate, was actually pretty considerate of her.

Wait, when she said she wanted to live here, was that so I wouldn't feel as obligated on the salary front? I never would have guessed she was thinking that far ahead from the start!

"Thank you, Rit."

"Eh? Um, you're welcome?"

Rit was likely playing dumb. I should've expected nothing less from the adventurer who took on Zoltan's problems completely solo. I decided to leave it at that, though, and just thanked her one more time in my heart.

*   *   *

I was walking beside Rit as we headed to a furniture store in search of a bed.

During the summer in Zoltan, it was well understood that you worked during the morning and evening. Midday was for relaxing and not causing a fuss. Because of that, despite it still being early, the streets were alive with people. Everyone was sweating and had annoyed expressions, though, so it wasn't quite the standard image of a bustling little town.

"Are you already used to Zoltan, Rit?"

"You mean this sort of mood? Yeah, though on a few levels it was pretty shocking at first. Is it like this everywhere with a hot climate?"

"No, even in other subtropical places, like Mzali, the silver town. There, miners head out to the mountains in search of ore in the morning. By noon, the town's bustling with all the places making lunch for the miners. At night, the people who are done working for the day are out drinking and carousing. It's a really lively town."

"You've been to Mzali?"

"To get mithril ingots, yeah. I've been lots of places, but I never would have guessed I would end up coming to Zoltan."

Zoltan had only sent a small amount of funds to Central for help in the battle against the demon lord's army and had hardly sent any soldiers. The frontier settlement didn't have any notable local specialties, was relatively underdeveloped technologically, and there weren't any particularly strong monsters around, either. The mountains in Central were crawling with owlbears, but out here a B-rank adventurer was needed to take care of just one of the creatures. That was proof enough of just how little the adventurers here knew when it came to fighting powerful enemies.

"Meaning it's peaceful. It's a land that doesn't need the Hero. A place that a member of the Hero's party, like me, would have no connection with. At least, that's what I thought at the time."

"A country that doesn't need the Hero. Yeah, that's true."

A half-elf girl was sitting on a window ledge with her feet in a bucket of water. She waved when she noticed me. If I remember correctly, I had given her some medicine when she had fallen and scraped her knee once.

"Sometimes…I used to feel like something was missing," Rit said as she watched the girl wave.

"Oh?"

"I didn't stay with your party. If I had traveled with you, I'm sure I would have been satisfied with that choice, too, but...being here with you now is what I would rather have."

"..."

There definitely could've been a path where Rit joined Ruti's group on the journey to defeat the demon lord. But that wasn't how it ended up. Instead of walking the path of the Hero through a storm of blood, we were walking together through Zoltan as just Rit and Red.

*   *   *

Stormthunder's Furniture Shop. An admittedly unusual name, but it was home to a skilled furniture craftsman.

"Are you there, Stormy?" Rit called out.

A short, stout figure emerged from somewhere deeper in the establishment. He had a nose like a boar and stood slightly shorter than a human, but he was well-built and broad-shouldered. The fangs sticking out of his mouth only served to reinforce his frightening appearance.

"Oh, Miss Rit. I'm always happy to have your patronage...but why is Red here with you today?"

"Uh, well it's a bit complicated," I responded.

Stormy—Stormthunder—was a bit confused at the unexpected pairing of the town's top adventurer and the medicinal herb-gathering specialist.

"I'm going to be moving in with Red starting today."

"Huh?"

"So I came to buy a bed."

"O-ohhhh, c-congratulations? I had no idea! Red's quite the lucky man."

"Wait, aren't you misunderstanding something?" I interjected.

"So you'd like to order a bed, then? Please leave it to me," Stormthunder said obsequiously as he focused on Rit.

"Oy, Storm, this is different from how you treated me before."

"That's because a certain customer bought a cheap bed after haggling over the price for thirty minutes. Another certain customer bought a high-grade bed at asking price! You're damn straight they don't get treated the same!" Stormthunder snapped back in exasperation.

"...Yeah, I guess so."

I couldn't really say anything else to that. It's not like he was wrong.

Stormthunder was a half-orc—a race with both human and orc heritage. In this case, half-orc didn't mean that one parent was human and the other was a full-blooded orc, but rather, they were mostly human but had an ancestor somewhere in the past who was an orc, and though diluted, orc blood still ran through them.

Orcs were a very belligerent race with boar-like faces from the dark continent and formed a key part of the demon lord's army. The orc hussars often used as advance forces in the invasion of Avalon were particularly infamous for their mobility and ravenous tendencies that led to them pillaging the countryside far and wide.

The orcs that Ruti and I first fought were orc hussars, as a matter of fact.

Whenever a war broke out between the two continents, there were many children of orc hussars born on this continent, too. Despite being born of such merciless and fierce stock as the advance troops of a fiendish army, half-orcs generally had the same sort of disposition as humans. However, because of their unpleasant appearances and origins, many were forced to live among the worst of society. Most worked as low-level enforcers in the criminal underworld or made a living as pillaging, mercenary outlaws.

Stormthunder's actual name was a word in the language of the dark continent that meant both storms and lightning, but he went by Stormthunder here to fit in with the language. The rest of the people in this part of town and I just called him Storm, though he didn't seem particularly fond of that nickname.

"So then, what are the dimensions of the room where you're putting this bed?"

The half-orc was bent over and taking an extremely fawning stance, the likes of which I had never seen before. Feeling like I had just gotten a small glimpse of the reality of a blue-collar craftsman who was usually so stubborn and mouthy, I glanced away and perused the furniture on display around the shop.

It was all made of wood, ranging from plain to intricately designed. There were pieces made of stout oak, beautiful ebony, and even rare ironwood. Most eye-catching of all was a bed made of livingwood, a material boasting extraordinary vitality. Even after it had been crafted into furniture, if you sprayed it with water, it would be able to naturally mend any scratches or nicks.

It was popular among the middle classes because of its long life span, but it was incredibly difficult to craft with. Working with the wood required the rare skill Intermediate Furniture Making. Such a luxury was not something that could normally be had in a town the size of Zoltan.

"Oy! If you aren't gonna buy anything, then get your hands off the goods!" Stormthunder had noticed me tapping the livingwood bed frame.

"Even if it gets a scratch, it can just heal, right?"

"That doesn't give you an excuse to go scratching it!" he shouted.

I just shrugged and backed away like he wanted. After a little bit, Rit called me over.

"I decided on this double bed made of walnut."

"Make it a single."

"Wuss...," Stormthunder muttered under his breath.

When I glanced at him sharply, he immediately looked away and said "I've got a single in the same design" as he fled to the back of the shop.

"Wuss," Rit said with a smirk, though she was blushing, too.

"It's only the second day since we met again," I said, deciding not to put too fine a point on it.

...A double bed? Seriously?

I honestly had no clue about things like that. I didn't have any experience there.

*   *   *

"There are more half-orcs in Zoltan than I would have guessed."

The bed was to be delivered in the evening. We had taken a statue, several paintings, plus a nice desk and table set from the estate Rit had been living in and were carrying them on a cart. An earth spirit beast that Rit had summoned pulled the load.

Rit's residence was extravagant, befitting the number one adventurer in town. It had four bedrooms, a private bar, a hidden door leading to a secret room, and a hidden passage out in case of an emergency. It also boasted a separate washroom and laundry; even the bath was pretty spacious.

Apparently, going forward, the two people she had employed to take care of the manor would continue living there, and she would open it up for merchants to rent out for gatherings and the like. The thought that such a venture was probably going to earn her a lot more money than the salary I was paying was a little disheartening.

"Red?"

"Hmm? Ah, sorry, what were you saying?"

"Come on. I was saying there are a lot of half-orcs in Zoltan."

It was true—there was a bit of a higher proportion of them here than in other countries.

"Stormthunder has the Craftsman blessing and a high level, but he ended up out here in Zoltan because he's a half-orc. They wouldn't let him open proper shops in other countries. He still gets dirty looks from a few people, but it doesn't go past that. A lot of the other halfs between humans and people from the dark continent come to Zoltan from other places looking for a reasonable environment to make a living in."

"I see… As expected, you knew everything right down to his blessing level."

"The truth is, I was short on money to pay for things I needed from him, so I've helped him out hunting before."

"Ah, so that's how it is. It's rough having a noncombat blessing."

There was no way to level a blessing up unless you fought and killed something else with a blessing. That was true whether you had a noncombat blessing or a Warrior blessing but made a living working at a job that had nothing to do with combat. The fundamental requirement in order to increase the power of your blessing was to wield a weapon and fight animals, monsters, or humans.

Divine Blessings.

With the exception of Asura demons, every living being in this world has that power from birth. The one who granted the Divine Blessing was Demis, the Almighty. God. On this continent, the worship of Demis was the state religion of every country. There were minor variations in the interpretations of the dogma, but the same basic tenets were followed by elves, dwarves, undeveloped tribes, goblins, and even by the few monsters that possessed intelligence.

This was because God granted everyone a power—Divine Blessings—that anyone could easily recognize, and because the presence of God could actually be felt through said blessing, there wasn't really much room for faith in other deities whose existences were less tangible.

To repeat myself, though, Divine Blessings were something bestowed on living things by God. They were not influenced in any way by parents or by how a child was raised. There were slum orphans born with Strategist and General blessings, and there had been nobles born with Thief blessings. What a child would be granted when it came into the world was something only God knew.

A Divine Blessing came with a name, skills associated with it, and levels. As its level increased, you were granted points that could be used to gain new skills; and by gaining skills, you could acquire superhuman strengths or techniques. Those new powers manifested in a myriad of fields beyond common knowledge. They ranged from straightforward abilities like magic, to deftness with a certain kind of weapon or armor, to the ability to create tools, to heart-moving singing. The majority of people judged the value of another by the level of their blessing.

It was fair to say that in order to attain great success, raising your blessing's level was a necessary first step. So then, how did you raise your blessing's level? There was just the one way: fight and kill an opponent who had a blessing of their own. Whether your blessing was meant for battle, that was the only method. Someone with a Craftsman blessing would never level up just from plying their trade.

Because of that, whether by hiring an adventurer to help with hunting to level up or by working as an adventurer on the side or something else, every living being had to kill other living beings in order to enhance their blessing.

The reason a rough-and-tumble sort of gathering of people like the Adventurers Guild was able to have such relative organizational power and influence was because of the wide range of people from all walks of life who were members in order to act as adventurers on the side.

Glancing to the side, I saw two girls about thirteen years old walking down the street as a shimmering heat haze obscured them slightly. They were chattering cheerfully despite the heat, and on their backs were plain, simple spears; the iron blades still had a bit of dark-red blood on the ends that they had forgotten to wipe off.

This world was filled with conflict.

*   *   *

We got a set of tableware and a few other odds and ends for Rit at the general store. I was pretty pleased with myself, since it had been a fairly reasonable deal.

"We should head to the market, too. It's about time I restocked on ingredients."

"Okay. I want to eat a burger steak today."

"A burger steak, huh? Got it."

I still had plenty of eggs. I mentally ran over my list of ingredients as we perused the marketplace. After a ten-minute walk, we passed an abandoned lot where a house had been toppled by a storm around two years back. We could hear children crying and angry shouts.

"A fight?"

Every town has its troublemakers. It's always iffy whether an adult who doesn't know the story behind the argument should butt in on a fight between children...

"That voice... Tanta?"

It was indeed Gonz's nephew, the half-elf Tanta. Apparently, he was involved.

"An acquaintance?"

"I think so. I'm going to go take a look real quick."

The voices were coming from the abandoned lot. Peeking over, I could see a group of three and a group of two going at one another. The pair were half-elves, and the trio were all humans. Tanta was brawling it out with one of the human boys, but it didn't appear to be going well for him.

"A skill?"

It seemed as if the human boy had managed to connect with his blessing. A precocious one, probably. He had already leveled up once or twice, and I could guess at the kind of blessing just by watching him fight.

I wanted to stop it. Looking closer, Tanta's opponent was the only one who really looked like he wanted to brawl. His two companions were content to just cheer from the sideline. Though, even they looked scared and were being careful not to get caught up in the middle of the fray.

That one human boy was probably the instigator.

"Oy, cut it out!" I called.

All the children swung around toward me. They looked a little scared to see an adult show up. Doubtless, they expected to get scolded, but they also seemed a little relieved. All except...

"Piss off!"

The boy who was beating up on Tanta reached down, picked up a stone, and threw it at me all in one fluid motion. Probably because of the Makeshift Fighting Technique skill.

There was a clang as I deflected the stone with my bronze sword. The children's eyes went wide, even those of the boy who threw it.

"Huh."

Unexpectedly, I found myself a little intrigued. That toss was no mere throw from a kid. There was a little tingle in my hand holding the sword. That had been a sharp attack.

"That sort of strength is overkill for a children's quarrel. You should try going out with an adult to fight some monsters."

"S-screw you! Talking all big when you've got a bronze sword!" The boy's face turned red as he shouted, and he quickly ran off.

"W-wait, Ademi!"

"Don't leave us behind!"

Ademi's cohorts chased after him. I just sighed slightly as I put my sword away. Honestly, I hadn't intended to draw my weapon. I thought I would knock it away with my hand. Had I done so, though, I probably would've hurt myself. Apparently, that kid had pretty good affinity with his blessing. Despite having only just awoken to it and still being a child, his attack was already a match for an E-rank adventurer.

"Are you okay, Tanta?"

"...Yeah."

Tanta looked frustrated as he rubbed his dirty face with his sleeve. The sleeve was dirty, too, though, so all it did was spread the mess.

"Look this way."

I used a towel I had with me to wipe off Tanta's face and then the other half-elf boy's face. The dirt was gone, but there was still a bit of bruising.

"There, all done."

"Thank you..."

"You were unlucky there, fighting a kid who had already connected with his blessing. Neither of you have connected yet, right?"

The two of them nodded sheepishly.

"But at low levels, it's not supposed to be that different from not having a blessing."

"He had an affinity with his blessing. For better or for worse."

"Affinity?" Tanta asked.

"Affinity is—," I started to try to explain.

"Uh, um!" the other boy interjected. He had fluffy, frizzy hair. His face was slightly rounder than Tanta's, though he had a bit of a droopy expression. His eyes were a little bloodshot, probably from trying to hold back tears.

"Wh-who is this, Tanta?" the boy asked.

"Ah, sorry, Al. He's Red, my friend the apothecary."

"An apothecary?"

"He's an adventurer, too."

"Oh, that's why he was so strong."

The boy was named Al, apparently. I thought I knew most of the kids from this part of town by now, but this was the first time I'd seen him.

"Big Bro, Al's family lives in the Southmarsh district."

"Ah, a Southmarsh kid. That explains why I haven't seen him around before."

Southmarsh was a residential district in western Zoltan. It was established by reclaiming marshland, making it not very popular as a residential area because of the uneven and soft ground. It had naturally come to be viewed as a slum for people who had come from outside Zoltan without much money. Perhaps realizing that, Al looked down when Tanta introduced him as being from Southmarsh.

"Oh, you hurt your knee."

It was Al's kneecap. There was red blood oozing out. He had probably gotten hurt after being pushed over. I took some disinfectant and a bandage out of my pocket.

"I need some water to take care of this, too. Can you walk to the well?"

"I-I'm fine. It's not that bad."

Al's face twitched in pain as I took his hand to help him move. The cut was probably deeper than it looked.

"No need to hold back," I said as I lifted Al onto my back and started walking.

"Whoa. Wah!" Al shouted. "I-I'm fine. I can walk on my own!"

He wriggled around, but I didn't pay it any mind as I carried him.

✳   ✳   ✳

"That'll do."

I had finished applying the medicine and then wrapped the leg to keep the sore areas stable and fixed in place.

"If you take it easy for two or three days, it should stop hurting."

"Thank you, Mr. Red."

Al smiled bashfully as I patted his head.

"Big Bro! What's going on on?!" Tanta shouted excitedly, in stark contrast to Al's quietness.

That wasn't too surprising, though…

"Why are you with Miss Rit?" Tanta asked.

"About that…"

"Because I'm friends with Red," Rit chimed in.

"Really?!"

"Really. We're going to be living together starting today."

"Eh?! Is he really dependable enough for something like that?"

"Hmm, well, I am a little bit concerned, truth be told…"

What did Rit think she was saying? She had no right to give kids strange ideas about me. Tanta shouldn't have been saying weird things, either! How did they think that made me feel?

"Um," Al nervously tried to speak up.

"Hmm? What is it, Al?"

"It's about Divine Blessings… You and Miss Rit know a lot about them, right?"

"I know a bit," I responded.

"It's about the guy who was fighting with us. His name is Ademi."

"You want to know about his?"

"Yes, sir. He was never that pleasant to be around and always hated elves, but he wasn't ever that violent before. But he suddenly changed a couple of days ago..."

"I see. That's probably because he connected with his blessing recently."

"Do people always end up like that when they make contact with their blessing?" Al's eyes wavered uneasily.

Blessings were a gift from God and essential in order to go through life in this world...

"Do you know what it means to make contact with your blessing?"

"Yeah! It means becoming conscious of what it is and being able to choose and develop your skills yourself, right?" Tanta eagerly cut in from the side.

I patted his head. He grabbed my hand with both of his and smiled happily.

"Correct. You've studied up."

"That much is just common knowledge."

"And when a person makes contact with their blessing, their personality is influenced by it."

"What do you mean?" Tanta tilted his head in confusion.

"For example, someone with the Craftsman blessing might start to like making things, or someone with the Mage blessing might start to be more interested in learning more. You could maybe say that a person's self-image is pulled in certain directions by their blessing."

"So that was what made Ademi so short-tempered?" The unease and fear was plain on Al's face.

Ah, so that's it...

"Have you reached the stage of becoming conscious of your blessing?"

"Y-yes, sir... I have the Weapon Master blessing."

"Ohhh, that's amazing."

Weapon Master was a blessing in the Warrior tree that mastered how to handle a single type of weapon. A weapon master sacrificed flexibility in being able to use different weapons situationally. In exchange, their obsession meant that the techniques they mastered far surpassed those that a warrior at a similar level could achieve with the same weapon. It was more suited for adventurers or soldiers who fought from a single base, rather than a traveling adventurer who wandered around gathering new weapons one after the other.

"That boy probably has the Bar Brawler blessing."

"Bar Brawler?"

"It focuses on unarmed combat, particularly in one-versus-many situations. It has innate skills related to using non-weapon items like stones or beer bottles as makeshift weapons, throwing and tripping opponents in order to get an upper hand, stuff like that. A weapon master who is dependent on their weapon and limited to an unarmed quarrel probably couldn't beat a bar brawler."

"That's why he suddenly got so good at fighting..."

"And the problem is that Ademi has an affinity for his blessing."

"An affinity?"

"Yeah. When a person's body and mindset are already well suited for their blessing, their skills become even stronger. Ademi might well be a genius bar brawler."

"A genius bar brawler...is kind of...not great."

"Yeah, that's sort of the problem. For blessings that are socially acceptable, it would be one thing, but for antisocial blessings like Thief, Bandit, Manslayer, and the like, having an affinity can be like a curse. It's the same for Ademi. With the Bar Brawler blessing, whenever there are obstacles in his path, his blessing will lead him to try to resolve them by fighting."

"I see... Um, is Weapon Master okay?"

"Well, compared to Bar Brawler, it's probably fine, but it can manifest in a misplaced and deep-rooted conviction about weapons. Not being able to relax without your weapon at hand, getting indignant if someone makes fun of it, etcetera."

"Ugh..." Al looked uneasy again.

That much was just everyone's lot in life, or perhaps it could be said that these were the roles that God expected us to fill...

"Well, you don't need to get that worried about it. It's true that blessings have a strong influence, but it's not like you have to be ruled by them, either. Once he gets used to it, Ademi will be able to control how he feels. You'll likely be able to keep it to a level where you just cherish your weapon."

"I don't even want a blessing," Al said.

Tanta's face stiffened at that. Rit's expression also turned pretty serious.

A Divine Blessing was God's chosen gift. To reject that was blasphemy. If an inquisitor of the holy church heard Al, it would be punishable as such. For a child, it would just be the whip and a scolding, but any older, such statements would only draw even more unwanted attention.

That said…I could sympathize with an unease toward your blessing. It was perfectly reasonable. I mean, I'm sure it wasn't just me, either. Rit's Spirit Scout, a blessing normally for filling the role of a scout for people of the forest, was the same.

Part of the reason she couldn't just behave herself in the castle might well have been the influence of a blessing so given to a free spirit. There was no telling whether Tanta had been granted a blessing that matched a job as a carpenter. Doubtless, the boy awaited the day he would make contact with his blessing with a mixture of anticipation and dread.

I didn't want to just bluntly contradict Al, though. If I tried to reject it off the cuff, he might take it the wrong way. A slipup here might've warped the kid's path in life. I was at a bit of a loss for what to say.

"Al, I agree it's a scary thing to come to terms with your blessing. It's almost like your life is completely decided by it. But you know, whatever blessing you might have, you'll still always be you," I said.

"What do you mean?"

"Your blessing is just one part of you. Just like your kind mother might have a side to her that nags and yells about little things, or your father might have a side to him that is totally different when he's drunk."

"Yeah, my father is usually scary, but when he drinks, he's always cheerful and smiling."

"All those different sides are a part of you. And your blessing is like that, too. When it feels like you might get carried away by your blessing, instead of rejecting it or becoming a slave to it, you should control it. It's one part of you, not the whole. If you can do that, your blessing will surely help you out a lot in the future."

"Really?"

"Really. The Weapon Master blessing allows you access to skills that increase your physical abilities and even grants you Immunity to Fear and Immunity to Confusion as long as you have your weapon in hand."

"Fear? E-everyone made fun of me for being scared of dark places... It can cure that?"

"Yeah. You won't be scared, no matter how dark it is."

Al looked just a little bit relieved as he smiled.

"Thank you, Big Bro Red."

"You're welcome. I'm usually at my apothecary, so if something is ever bothering you, feel free to come by anytime. If you don't mind hanging with a D-rank adventurer, I'd be happy to talk things through with you."

"Yeah! ...Um."

"What? Something still on your mind?"

"Is it okay if I come by, even if I don't have anything that's bothering me?" Al's face got slightly red as he met my eyes.

"Of course you can. Come have something to eat, too," I responded, tousling his soft, frizzy hair.

"Okay!"

Al flashed a beaming, childlike grin. I couldn't help noticing the dimple that formed when he smiled.

✳   ✳   ✳

Because we took a bit of a roundabout path, it was already almost noon by the time we reached the market. Rit and I were sweating as we gathered the food.

"I got everything on my list," she said.

"All right."

I had split the things I wanted to get into two lists and given Rit one. The merchants at the market were not even trying to call out to draw people in. Perhaps the heat had robbed them of the energy. They were just fanning themselves from the shade of their stores. Thankfully, that meant no one tried to call us over, either, so we didn't have to waste any time, which was good. Still, I couldn't help a bit of a wry smile at the Zoltan-esque laziness of it all.

It seemed like Rit had a similar reaction, enjoying the experience for her part, since she didn't usually go to the market.

"In Loggervia, the market is annoying, even in summer. Merchants would always start with pre-written spiels about how 'Summer fatigue is a thing of the past ever since I started eating this every day,' and all that rubbish."

"My hometown was rural, so it didn't even have a market. Various homes making different things and just gathering together to trade was all."

"So that was what your hometown was like? But didn't you leave to join the knights by the time you were eight?"

"Yeah. My only memories of my home are from when I was a little boy."

Thanks to that, I wasn't the kind of person who was particularly attached to my hometown. In fact, I was away from it for so long that there were times I even wondered if Ruti would forget about me... But the handful of times a year I came back, my little sister was always the first person to come out to the entrance of the village to greet me, faster than anyone else.

"Heh, that sure is nostalgic."

But now she was getting along so well with Ares. I had never even noticed it developing.

"...I can't really believe that."

"Hmm?"

"I can't imagine her ever opening up to anyone other than you, Red."

"Really?"

"Yeah. I don't know anyone as scary as she is."

"Scary?" For a moment, I thought Rit might've been joking, but the young blond woman's expression was serious.

"When I faced off against her in the arena, it was the first time I realized what it meant to have goose bumps. Fighting her there was the scariest thing I've ever done. Scarier than any demon. So when I saw her fawning over you, Red—no, I should use your old name. When I saw her fawning over Gideon, I just couldn't believe it."

"Huh. Well, she definitely can be a bit hard to read."

"I can't begin to imagine her acting like that with Ares instead of with you."

That was pretty high praise, but it seemed like Rit genuinely doubted the possibility. Honestly, even I was a bit worried about how my sister was doing, but…

"Well, Ruti is far stronger than me now. I don't know where the Hero's party is, but apparently, they defeated the heavenly king of the wind, so they're probably getting along fine."

"…That's true! We're out here in Zoltan, so even if we got worried about things, there's not much we could do about it," Rit said as she took my arm, as if trying to take my mind off the trail it was on.

"Let's head back."

"Yeah, let's."

Far removed from the battle that would decide the fate of the world, we were in an entirely different realm, so distant from the Hero's party.

▶ ▼ ▼ ◀ ◀

Interlude

- - - - - - - -

Ruti the Hero Was Alone

▶ ▲ ▲ ▲ ◀

"Get it together, Ares! How many times has it been now?!" growled
Danan, a member of the Hero's party and bearer of a Martial Artist
blessing.

"If we're out, then we can just go back and buy more, can't we?" Ares
the Sage responded, seemingly unperturbed by his companion's anger.
His lips trembled slightly despite the rebuke, a clear indication that he,
the Sage, felt humiliated at being scolded like a child by an uneducated
man like Danan.

Currently, the Hero's party was in the Desert of Bloody Sands
searching for a weapon that had been left there by the previous demon
lord. Their goal was to either get their hands on it or destroy it before
the current demon lord's army could make it their own. However, this
was the third time they had needed to return to a settlement because
they had run out of food and water. Part of it was just that they did not
know where the weapon was, and searching took time, but there had
also been a clear increase in the number of times they had run out of
supplies in the middle of their journeys ever since Gideon—Red—had
left the party.

"How much time do you think we've wasted in this desert going
back to the same place?! The reason we couldn't get the help of the desert people is because you screwed up the negotiations!"

"It's a legendary weapon. It's not something anyone could find by just spending a day or two looking. And I did my best with the negotiations, but the desert peoples were no better than thieves who wouldn't even obey the king of their land. If you've got complaints, though, then feel free to do it yourself next time," Ares said with a shrug.

Ares's confident and dismissive attitude only served to further aggravate Danan.

"You're the one who said you'd take care of gathering supplies and doing the negotiations in Gideon's stead! Where's that big talk now?!"

"Unlike Gideon, I can't spend all my time doing odd jobs," Ares responded casually. To him, Danan was getting angry over inconsequential details, but when he noticed Danan's expression turn dead serious, a danger signal flashed in the back of his mind. By then, it was too late.

"Screw it. I'm going to go find Gideon. We won't get anywhere at this rate."

"Wait a minute! We're headed to the previous demon lord's secret facility! If you leave now, we'll be down a man should a fight break out!"

"At this rate, we're just going to get wiped out anyway. I only joined this party because I thought it was the most direct route to beating the demon lord. If that's no longer true, then there's no point in me being here." Danan was serious. Or at the very least, he looked that way to Ares. He glanced at the Crusader, Theodora, looking for some help, but she just closed her eyes and crossed her arms as if it had nothing to do with her. Tisse, the assassin who had joined in Gideon's place, was faithful to Ares, since he had hired her, but she would not be of any help in a situation like this.

"Pushing Gideon out was a grave mistake, Ares. You were too hasty."

"Like I've said every time now, I didn't push him out. He said it himself." Ares's excuse did nothing to change the sneer on Danan's scarred face.

At that moment, though…

"Are you going to go look for my brother, Danan?" a cool voice rang out. One cold enough to freeze Danan's sneer.

"Milady, I…" Danan, whose body was encased in the armor of his own muscle, shrank back, as if cowering before a single little girl. It was a similar response to the panic that prey might experience when a megapredator it had no chance of defeating or escaping was staring it down. The Hero, Ruti. Her small body was wrapped in platinum armor, and the Holy Demon Slayer sword hung at her waist as she looked up at the bear of a man, expressionless…

She was the strongest being chosen by God. The Hero who had been granted supernatural strength in order to save the world. Even a martial artist like Danan, who could tear steel apart with his bare hands, understood instinctively that he could not win against her.

Danan swallowed nervously.

"I-if we leave things to Ares any more than this, the party will fall apart. We need your brother, Gideon. Even you…"

"Even I, what?"

"N-no, nothing…" It was no good. Danan's knees started to buckle. It was all he could do to resist the impulse to break eye contact with her. Even just that was enough to grind down the mental fortitude of a man who had lived through hundreds of life-and-death battles. It was only a brief silence, but to Danan, it may as well have been hours.

"I'll allow it. Go."

"Eh?"

"Danan, go in search of Gideon. We will continue the journey."

"W-wait, that's…"

"That is all." With that, Ruti retired to her personal tent.

She alone had a personal tent because she was the party's leader, but the real reason was because not even Ares could endure being in a cramped tent with her. Excepting for when they were adventuring, Ruti generally just did things on her own. The only exception to that had been Gideon.

"P-please, wait a minute, Ruti!" Ares desperately chased after the young woman.

Danan breathed a deep sigh and sat himself across from Theodora, who still had her eyes shut.

"So what will you do?" Theodora asked.

"There's nothing I can do but go," Danan responded with a shrug. "Even though I prided myself on being the cornerstone of the party's attack."

"Second to the Hero, you mean."

"Well yeah, she's on a whole other level. I can't believe there was really a time when she was weak."

"Everyone starts out weak when their blessing's level is low... But I agree. Though Ares might know more about her from back then, since he was in the party from the start."

"Ares, huh...?" Perhaps because he had finally calmed down, Danan reverted to his usual insolent tone. Rubbing the scar on his cheek, Danan lowered his voice a bit. "Do you think there's anything to the idea that he killed Gideon for getting in his way?"

"Hmm."

"I don't think there's any question he wants to marry the Hero. He's the son of a failed duke, and the family is clinging to what status it has left. I'm sure he has dreams of reviving his family's title. If the Hero and the Sage who saved the world became a couple, they could rally a lot of support. He might even be able to parlay that into carving out a duchy all his own to rule... There might be something to what Yarandrala was saying."

After Gideon had disappeared, Yarandrala, a high elf, had pushed Ares on the matter. Her blessing was the Singer of the Trees, which allowed her to control plants. Right after Gideon disappeared, she had used that to investigate any traces of his whereabouts but turned up nothing.

In truth, Gideon had known of her ability and had taken steps to disappear without her being able to find him. To Yarandrala, it just made the situation feel all the more unnatural. She suspected that Ares had attacked Gideon for blocking his way to glory. When the elf grabbed the Sage by the collar and hounded him about it, Ares broke his promise to Gideon and even went so far as to say that Gideon had deserted them.

High elves were not known for being short-tempered, but they were passionate. They would not get angry over nothing, but when they did, it was a blazing rage. After hearing Ares's words, Yarandrala did not hesitate in the least, slugging him in the face then and there.

Ares was incredibly prideful. When she punched him, he flew off the handle and immediately fired back with his magic, and Yarandrala fired back with her own. It was a battle between two blessings at the pinnacle of the mage line. The Sage and the high-level spirit mage blessing of the Singer of the Trees. Ares brought a meteorite crashing down with his Meteor spell, and Yarandrala called forth a Tyrant Spirit, summoning a wooden giant that could shrug off the incoming meteorite. If Danan and Theodora had not cut in to separate them, the local geography would have been drastically altered, for sure.

"I can't understand you people" was the last thing Yarandrala had said before leaving the party.

"Yarandrala was crying," Danan muttered, thinking back to the day the high elf had left.

"…She was."

After Yarandrala left, Danan and Theodora had blamed Ares's short temper. Both for pushing Gideon out and for getting into a fight with Yarandrala. Because of him, they had lost two comrades. But Ares had merely tried to brush it off as Yarandrala's personality having always been a problem. That evasion pushed Danan beyond anger, dumbfounding him.

If Yarandrala were with them, their search would be much easier thanks to her ability to control plants. But that line of thought just started stoking Danan's anger again. He quelled the fury with another sigh.

The man thought back to what she had said at the time. Since he was going to be looking for Gideon now, he could not help but consider that possibility. Ares had said that Gideon ran away, but it was not as if there was any proof that Ares hadn't killed him. Danan recalled the menacing look on Yarandrala's face. If Ares had actually admitted to killing Gideon there, either he or Yarandrala would probably have died in the ensuing fight. It was possible Ares just said what he had as a desperate excuse. Had he really killed Gideon, then Danan's new journey would never end.

Faced with the unusual sight of Danan's troubled face, Theodora smiled slightly.

"Sir Gideon is truly skilled at battle. I'm amazed he could fight at the level he did with nothing more than common skills."

"I feel the same. I always thought he was a tactician worthy of respect."

"That didn't seem to stop you from always criticizing him for mistakes in combat."

Danan shuddered with a start. The insolent man's shoulders drooped as if ashamed of himself.

"I... That's just the sort of personality I have... I can't settle down if I don't call a mistake what it is... But I can swear on my Divine Blessing, I never once thought Gideon wasn't critical to our party, let alone that he was anything like a burden holding us back."

"Then maybe you should have actually let him know that."

"...Which means you think Gideon left on his own?"

Theodora snapped the stick she was holding in her hands and tossed the two pieces into the fire.

"Sir Gideon is a man that both you, the greatest martial artist of our times, and I, the assistant instructor of the temple knights' style of spear wielding, have acknowledged. No matter how skilled a magic user Ares may be, would a swordsman respected by two of the pinnacles of physical combat really be so quickly overpowered in a one-on-one versus a mage?"

"That's right!" the martial artist exclaimed.

There had been a bit of an inflection in Theodora's words, as though she was trying to convince herself, too. Danan could recognize that.

Gideon must still be alive. He was a comrade we trusted with our backs countless times, in dozens of do-or-die situations. If we're still alive, then he should be, too.

There was no way he would die on them.

"Tch, if that's how it was, I should have gone looking for him sooner. Then we wouldn't have had to deal with this pain-in-the-ass desert."

"Yes, if I had said something sooner, I could have been the one to go out looking for him."

The two of them looked at each other and exchanged smiles.

Chapter 4

- - - - - - - - -

Zoltaŋ's Rit

The day after, we went shopping.

As I made breakfast for the two of us, I thought back to how much my day-to-day life had changed in the past couple weeks. I had been living in a cheap little town house in the blue-collar part of town, but now I had the apothecary of my dreams. The princess who had been one of my companions back in the day had forced her way into my home and was living with me, and here I was in the kitchen, making breakfast for two.

"Life's a strange thing."

If someone had asked me way back whether I could have imagined a future like this, the answer would have most definitely been no. I could have seen a future fighting against the demon lord with Ruti in the Hero's party, or a future keeping the capital's peace as the second-in-command of the Bahamut Knights, or even a future where I became a noble with a modest amount of land covering the village where I was born and the surrounding territory... But running an apothecary with a princess in Zoltan of all places...

"Not that this is bad, though."

I set the food on the two plates. Drawn by the scent, Rit jerked herself up from bed, still looking sleepy.

"Breakfast."

Rit being with me and saying things like that with her carefree smile had already become a small source of happiness for me.

*　　　　　*　　　　　*

We had taken care of pretty much all the shopping yesterday, which meant that today was:

"Taking care of the approval for Red's medicine."

"I'm not a big fan of calling it that, though. Doesn't red medicine evoke a dangerous sort of feeling?"

Crimson medicine, a red drug. No matter how you put it, it sounded foreboding.

"Then how about Redrit medicine? Which reminds me, we need to get the store's sign changed."

"Were you serious about changing it to Red & Rit's Apothecary? If we change the store's name, you can't go quitting on me later, you know," I joked.

"Does that mean you'll have me stay here forever?" Rit fired back with a playful grin.

"Okay, I get it. We can go by the sign shop, too," I responded with a smile. "That and the approval for the new anesthetic. I already bought the silver tableware for the gift, so all that's left is to head over."

"It would be better to have a letter of introduction, but I can use my connections to take care of that side of things."

"How like you, Rit, always on top of things. Thanks, that will help." In such a situation, it was best that I just accepted the help the blond girl offered. Rit was the top adventurer in Zoltan, so she had a lot of clout.

"You're better at the actual negotiations, though, right?"

"Yep, leave it to me."

*　　　　　*　　　　　*

I had felt confident about my ability to work out an agreement, but…

"Absolutely not!"

I was rejected point-blank. There wasn't even any room for negotiations.

Dan, a middle-aged man with a bit of a gut, was the official working for the council that adjudicated the approval of new medicines. Maybe he was tired, but his face seemed haggard despite being a bit chubby, and there were bags under his eyes.

"Please, wait. My medicine is a safe alternative with reduced dependence. Can't we at least talk this through a bit first?"

"I don't need to talk anything through. Take your gift and leave!"

Up until after he had taken the letter of introduction from the high-level bureaucrat that Rit knew, Dan had maintained a business smile, even if he couldn't totally hide his lack of interest. But as soon as I started to talk about the actual point of the visit—the medicine—his attitude changed dramatically.

"Is there some kind of problem?"

"I-it's got nothing to do with you."

I knew the official's sudden change in mood wasn't because of us. The shift only happened after he heard we were there to get approval for a new medicine. From that, it wasn't hard to guess something was up, but the crucial point of why he refused the application wasn't clear.

I should have gathered a bit more information beforehand.

I never would have guessed it would end up like this, and I didn't know anything about Dan. Even if I tried to negotiate, I didn't have any sort of position from which to attack.

Huh, am I getting complacent after leaving the front lines? I've lost my edge.

Living a life as someone who just gathered herbs every day had definitely worn away at some of my capabilities. Skills granted by a blessing could never be lost, but your own ability to judge when and how to use them definitely dulled without regular practice.

After Rit had gone to all that trouble to get me a letter of introduction, it was a shame for it to go to waste, but there wasn't anything we could do. We left the reception office.

"What was that about?!" Rit wondered, indignant.

Actually, there was a moment in there where she was seething and seemed about ready to grab Dan by the collar. If I hadn't held out a hand to stop her, and also taken the reins by asserting our position, Rit might have resorted to using her strength to wring an approval out of the poor man. Despite growing up a princess, she was the kind of person who had trouble finding the patience for lengthy discussions.

"I've really gotten weak. That wasn't something that could be resolved with negotiations."

The first thing I needed to do was investigate the real reason he had rejected us. It probably wouldn't take that long, but…having stepped away from those kinds of adventures already, it was honestly a pain in the ass.

"Then let's try asking his boss," Rit suggested.

"His boss? …Yeah, I guess so."

Right, I had Rit on my side. I'd just have to use her status as the top adventurer in these parts as much as I could.

✳   ✳   ✳

"It's an honor to have a visit from the one and only Miss Rit."

Rudolf, the head of the department in charge of rules and regulations regarding commerce and industry, was a man in the middle of his life with a bit of gray hair starting to show. He was smiling amiably, as if genuinely happy to meet the young adventurer.

"The truth is that I'm working with Red now, and there was something I wanted to ask about, if you didn't mind."

"Ohhh? Miss Rit, famous for her solo work, is teaming up? I can't wait to see what comes of it. Mr.…Red was it? It's an honor to meet you."

There was no need for me to mention here that I was a D-rank adventurer. I just flashed a vague smile as I took his outstretched hand.

"Anyway, we came to inquire about getting approval for the sale of a new drug to be used as an anesthetic, but we were rejected by the man in charge of overseeing the approval."

"Ah, I understand," Rudolf said, nodding apologetically. "I'm quite sorry about that, but your timing is a bit unfortunate for that sort of request."

"I guess something really has happened, then?"

"As expected of Miss Rit, I suppose. Yes, as you say, there's been a bit of a problem. It's not really something to be talking about where others might hear, so I'd like to ask you to keep this to yourselves."

"Of course."

Rit and I both nodded in affirmation before Rudolf continued.

"About a month ago, a medicine that Dan approved turned out to have a powerful narcotic effect if it was prepared slightly differently, and in the shadows, it has been spreading like wildfire among our poorest residents. Even some among the nobility have started using it."

"A drug that was approved a month ago?" I asked.

I was a little confused by that. Even though I was stocking my own medicines, I would have guessed Newman or one of the other doctors would have mentioned a new drug.

"I suppose you're familiar with medicines, Mr. Red? Even so, it's not surprising you wouldn't know about it. A large amount of the drug was prepared outside Zoltan before it was approved. As soon as the approval was granted, it was all brought in and then apparently immediately sold to people who had already reserved orders of it. The intent was to sell it as a narcotic from the very start, it seems."

"Really? It would seem like, after going to all that work to get the approval, selling it that way would obviously lead to regulation, even if it did earn a big initial profit. I would think a continuing stream of sales would be hard to maintain."

"Yes, it's quite the puzzle. Perhaps it's just the shortsightedness of a novice herbalist. Anyway, it has been quite the black eye and a bit of a problem for us, so Dan has been working day and night to deal with the fallout while receiving no small amount of reprimand himself."

That explained it, then. Secretly, I had been more than a little angry with that chubby man, but I was able to sympathize a bit more after having learned of his position. It must have been rough. I wanted to make a point of having the next medicine I came to him for approval be something to settle a nervous stomach.

"Since it's you making the request, Miss Rit, I'm sure there won't be a problem. Could you let me see the paperwork? I'll take care of the approval myself."

"Really?! Thank you very much!"

We ended up getting the approval rather easily from an unexpected source. Rit's influence was really something.

...I had known, of course, but it was still a little depressing. Back during my adventures, I had been in charge of negotiations. It stung a bit to know that this was all I could accomplish without the influence that came with being a member of the Hero's party.

We showed Rudolf the documents regarding the medicine, he double-checked that there weren't any problems, and he issued the official endorsement.

With that, I could at last sell my medicine without issue.

*   *   *

After leaving the council building, my shoulders slumped a bit as we walked.

"Sorry, all I could do was rely on you for everything."

Even though I had said I would take care of the negotiations myself, in the end, Rit had been the one who got it done. I couldn't help being a little disappointed in myself.

In response, the young woman, who walked ahead of me, turned around and shook her head.

"All I've done is rely on you for cooking. Does that bother you? Do you cook because you want me to apologize?"

"...Of course not."

"Red, I'm glad I could help you out. There's absolutely no reason to apologize. I'll help you as often as you need me to from now on. I'd do anything for you."

Mentally, I was rather taken aback at the unexpectedly straight-forward affection. Rit paused, too, while the two of us faced each other. I wasn't so uncouth as to ask her why she would go that far for me.

"Thank you, Rit. I... I, uh... I guess this means I'll be counting on you in the future as well."

"Yep!"

Drawn in by Rit's cheerful smile, I ended up smiling, too.

✳   ✳   ✳

"It will take a bit of time until word about the effects of the new medicine spreads," Rit said.

That night, we sat at the living room table, discussing how best to increase sales for the shop.

"Though, the first question is whether a new anesthetic will even sell at all," I added.

"Yeah, it would be good to have another drug with a more obvious effect that people would want to buy."

"That's easy to say, but..."

All I had was the first-tier preparation skill. There was a limit to the medicines I could prepare.

"I've got a wide breadth of knowledge but no specialized skills. There isn't a medicine I know of that fits such a convenient niche."

"Right..."

What I had that other apothecaries didn't was that I didn't have to worry about monsters while gathering herbs. I could also reach the mountain in a few minutes when it would otherwise take someone a day, maybe half a day if they had put a normal amount of points into a skill that increased movement speed. It was a big advantage, but without a difference in the medicines themselves, that wouldn't lead to a significant increase in sales.

"At most, it just helps when we actually run low on medicine," I muttered. In just one day, I could get more than enough of a supply ready to sell, and it would only take half a day if I limited my gathering to what was actually needed.

"Do you have any ideas?" I asked.

"Hmmmm," Rit mused, closing her eyes.

She was probably connecting with her blessing and checking again if there was anything she could do with the skills she had.

"We could try making a magic potion using spirit magic? I could work on it together with you."

"Yeah, that might be a possibility. If we advertised it as being made from your magic, it would probably sell among adventurers in Zoltan."

That said, Rit's blessing—Spirit Scout—was fundamentally in the Warrior tree. Its magic was more of a trump card, working best as a hidden ace up her sleeve.

"I know my magic isn't really that strong," Rit said, looking a little depressed.

She had probably noticed my expression. The blond girl was well aware that her magic was more supplementary than a main feature. That much was obvious from the fact that she used a two-sword style of fighting that occupied both her hands, even though she would have to use her fingers to make a seal to activate her magic skills.

"Other than that... Yeah, I've got nothing!" Rit raised both hands, throwing them up in a sign of defeat. Generally speaking, the skills provided by blessings were oriented toward battle. There were hundreds of different weapon skills, but the whole of making medicine was covered by a few tiers of Preparation skills—those being Elementary, Intermediate, and Advanced. It was a rather small number of ranks, despite such a wide variety of curatives.

Blessings were created for the purpose of conflict. That was what the holy church's clergy taught. If you asked me, that much was clear just from the breadth and depth of combat skills compared with the vaguer tier structure to productive skills. This meant that, when it came to medicine, unless we hired someone with Intermediate Preparation or higher, there wasn't much else we could do.

"It's a difficult thing to solve, even though your cooking is so good," Rit said.

She seemed to be enjoying snacking on the white radish and pickled octopus laid out on the table. Though the girl praised it heavily, all I did was boil the octopus before pickling it. Then I sprinkled some salt on the radish. It was because of my Cooking skill that even simple dishes turned out pretty well.

"Maybe that's it? Maybe you could sell food out of the apothecary?"

"Don't be silly. All I have is Elementary Cooking, and it's just level one at that. There's no way I could match up against a professional chef."

"With how good even this sort of cooking tastes, I think it would probably work."

"Serving food would mean a ton of extra work. You couldn't call this place busy, but it's not so little work that I can do an entirely different job at the same time, too."

"I guess so. Too bad," Rit responded, looking disappointed.

But an apothecary serving food... That was something I had never heard of. I started to laugh a little subconsciously, but then...

"An apothecary that serves food?" Something about what Rit said had piqued my interest, and I started thinking about it.

"What is it? Are you really considering running a restaurant, too?"

"No, not that... But there is something I want to try," I said as I stood up. Rit seemed interested, following along behind me while asking what I had hit upon.

I took some powdered immune-system-boosting herbs. Usually, the plant was used as a preventive against fatigue and sickness and was fairly effective in treating colds and other mild illnesses. However, its taste was extremely bitter. It was the kind of medicine you'd want to give children with weaker immune systems, but it wasn't uncommon for them to throw it back up after drinking it because of how awful it tasted.

I dissolved a little bit of the powder in some water and mixed it in with some apple jam. Then I took the jam and spread it around a pie crust and put it in the oven. Thanks to my Elementary Preparation skill, I could protect the active ingredient from the heat. And thanks to my Elementary Cooking skill, I could arrange the dish so the bitter taste of the medicine would help bring out the jam's sweetness. It took only ten minutes to bake the crust.

"I think I could use medicine as an ingredient in cooking!"

Rit looked utterly flummoxed; she hadn't considered such a thing before. I retrieved the golden-brown pie.

"How about a taste test to see how it worked," I offered as I cut the pie in half with a knife. It at least looked like a perfectly normal jam pie. Praying for a success, we each took a bite.

"It's pretty good!" Rit said.

"Yeah, the medicine's bitterness doesn't stick out at all like this."

This way, even a kid wouldn't have to feel like they were actually taking any awful-tasting medicine.

"With a pie, it won't keep very long, so maybe I should go with cookies? I'll give that a shot, too," I added.

"Then how about baking a bunch of smaller cookies to use for public taste tests? It's just a nutritional supplement and immune-system booster, so there shouldn't be any problem if healthy people ate them, too, right?"

"Yeah, that's a good idea."

"I'll go around handing them out tomorrow!"

The two of us locked hands happily. The next day was shaping up to be a fun one.

*   *   *

On the following day, Rit took a basket filled with cookies and spent a few hours handing them out to farmers and adventurers among the northern district and blue-collar parts of Zoltan. While she was doing that, I offered a taste test to the few customers who came by the store.

"The feedback was good!" she reported excitedly.

"Same here," I responded.

The two of us were beaming as we looked at each other. Whether we would actually be able to sell them was likely to take a while longer to know for sure, though. No sooner had the thought crossed my mind than the bell by the door rang.

"Pardon me."

"Welcome!"

A woman who looked a little tired came into the shop. Maribelle, her name was, if I recalled correctly. She was a mother from the laborer side of town.

"I heard that you had a medicine in the form of a cookie here..."

Could business have already been picking up?

"Yes, we do. At the moment, we have a nutrient-enhancement cookie that is effective against colds. Would you like to try a sample?"

"Oh, that bitter medicine..."

I offered her one of the small biscuits. After hesitating for a moment, she steeled herself and bit into it.

"?! That's good! My daughter might even be able to eat that without throwing up! Even if I mix the medicine with milk, she always has trouble keeping it down, so I was totally at a loss for what to do." Maribelle beamed, and then she added, "I'd like to buy some, please."

Apparently, news of the medicine spread quickly by word of mouth. Before nightfall, several customers had stopped in to buy some medicinal cookies.

"I'd like five, please."

"Of course," Rit answered.

Standing at the counter, she dexterously wrapped the cookies in bags. There were no more of the smaller taste-testing cookies left. But even without them, seeing one person after the other buying the little things made other customers want to get some, too, and in the blink of an eye, the cookies were selling expeditiously.

In only thirty minutes…

"I'm incredibly sorry, but that was the last of today's batch. We will be making more tomorrow, though, so please come again." Rit and I ended up apologizing to the customers as we held up the empty baskets.

Once all the customers had left, the two of us beamed at each other with looks of satisfaction. Then we high-fived.

The cookies were by no means incredibly profitable, but it was gratifying to be able to sell out completely like that. Plus, having so many customers in the shop, which was usually pretty empty, made it feel like I really was running my own business for the first time.

"That's Red for you! You really are amazing!"

"No, it was only thanks to your advice."

"Really? …I'm happy to hear that." Rit's face turned a little bit red. Something about how she looked was so cute. I couldn't help myself. I grabbed her and lifted her into the air.

"Wah?"

With my shop finally coming into its own, I was a bit over the moon.

"Thanks for being with me, Rit! If it wasn't for you, I would have just stayed bored and alone behind the counter in an apothecary that no one visited!"

I held Rit up and spun in a circle happily. I'd said something incredibly embarrassing, but at the time, it hadn't bothered me.

Despite being so assertive when she was making her own pitch, when I was the proactive one, Rit ended up flushing pink shades, not knowing what to do with herself.

"Y-yeah… I think I would have always been alone in Zoltan otherwise, so…I'm glad I could be with you," Rit mumbled as she turned crimson and hid her cheerful smile behind the blue bandanna around her neck.

Unfortunately for her, I was a battle-hardened former member of the Hero's party. My Perception skill was pretty high, so I didn't happen to have the kind of ears that would conveniently miss that line.

"I'm going to remember that, word for word," I said.

Rit's face turned a deeper red, and she fell silent in my arms. It was clear she was smiling, even though it was hidden beneath the bandanna. I could tell what she was feeling perfectly well, even without a mind-reading skill.

Interlude

- - - - - - - - -

Loggervia's Rizlet

Loggervia Castle, Rit's room.

"What do I do…?"

The princess sat hugging her knees. Her master, as well as the adventurers who she'd traveled with, were gone. They had been killed by the Asura demon, Shisandan.

The army looking to capture Loggervia Castle had stopped their offensive at the loss of their commander, but the castle was still surrounded by the demon lord's troops. Supply lines had been severed.

The gradual depletion of supplies, particularly the decreases in food and fuel, was having a significant impact on the morale of the castle's defenders. Loggervian winters were cold. Without fuel to burn to stay warm, many people would freeze to death. It went without saying what would happen without food.

Even if they held out, they couldn't win. The military might of the Duchy of Loggervia had suffered several diplomatic problems with their neighboring countries. In particular, they had gotten into a small-scale squabble with the nearby country of Sunland over the rights to a quarry near the border before the demon lord's army had invaded.

If Loggervia didn't lower its head and send out a letter pleading for reinforcements, they could not hope for help from the outside. But with them surrounded, no envoy would survive. On top of that, it was clear that the demon lord's army had more than enough supplies. The orcs who made up a significant chunk of the army were resistant to the cold of winter. Loggervia's frozen climate was an ally to their enemy.

In order to break out of that deadlock, Rit had tried to lead a force of Loggervian adventurers in a surprise attack against the enemy's main forces with the help of her master, Gaius, and his royal guard, but...

This is all I have to show for it...

Upon finding out that Gaius had already been killed, Rit's father, the country's sovereign, had fallen prey to depression. The two of them had been close friends from a young age. The reason he had left the education of his beloved daughter to Gaius was because of his confidence in Gaius's character. He blamed himself because, despite his long kinship with the man telling him something was off, he had not been able to see through the fact that someone had taken Gaius's place. That self-reproach and depression caused the leader of a dauntless military power to lose his will to fight.

It was the same for Rit, too. The fact that she had not realized the master she idolized had been replaced by someone else, that she had been deceived, and that she was responsible for so many people dying because of that had wounded her spirit.

I'm sorry. I'm sorry. I'm so sorry...

Even though they had gotten revenge by defeating Shisandan, Rit's heart was still shrouded in gloom, and all she could do was keep apologizing.

Then came a knock on the door.

* * *

I knocked on the door to Rit's room. I could sense her presence behind the door, but there wasn't a response.

"Rit, may I come in?"

"...Gideon?"

"Yeah, it's me."

"Sure…"

Opening the door, I saw Rit sitting on her bed. Her eyes were red and swollen from crying.

"Is it okay if I sit?" Seeing the girl nod, I sat down next to her on the bed. "Today's war council is over. Apparently, they intend to maintain the situation and hole up for a siege."

"Uh-huh."

"But everyone recognizes things will only get worse at this rate. With Gaius gone, the people are disorganized."

"It can't be helped."

Rit's expression was despairing, as if she'd already accepted the seemingly inevitable destruction of her home. The princess had given up, like so many others. At this rate, Loggervia really would be destroyed by the demon lord's army.

As an outsider, I was reluctant to intrude too much in other people's affairs, but I resolved myself to confront the blond girl.

"Rit."

"…"

"Rit! Look at me!"

I grabbed both her shoulders and forced her to face me. Her eyes were damp with tears as they met mine.

"I know you're hurting. I understand the country has lost its will to fight, too. But, Rit, you said you were going to protect this country, didn't you?"

"Yeah…"

"If you tell me now that you really don't want to fight anymore, I won't make you. But that isn't what this is. It's not that you don't want to fight. It's that the sadness is weighing you down."

"Maybe. But it's hopeless. The swords I loved so much… I can't even hold them anymore. I'm scared… I'm scared to lose anything else," she admitted as her tears started flowing again.

I gently drew her toward me, and she buried her face in my chest and started crying, unable to hold it back.

"…Scared. I'm so frightened… I knew the people who died. Clive had a wife. They only just got married last year, and he was always talking about how great his bride was. Danny had a sick father. He always worked so hard to pay for his father's medicine. Old man Soret was going to retire in another year. He said he was going to bake tons of cookies for his grandson once he retired. Bobby was an orphan who I helped once when he got involved with some delinquents. He ended up becoming an adventurer after that because he wanted to be like me. I…I…told him, 'Do your best; I-I'm sure you'll become a strong adventurer someday.' If I hadn't said that…he'd still be alive now. The royal guard and the adventurers…all of them… I…"

"They were good people."

"There were bad people, too. And folk somewhere in between. But I talked to them all. I knew their faces. I knew what sort of personalities they had! What sort of lives they led! Why they were willing to fight with me! I knew it all! But they're all gone now. Because of me, they're all dead. I'll never see them again. It's scary, and it's lonely." Rit sobbed.

Hugging her shoulders, I tried to share as much of the pain in her heart as I could. I felt her sobs as she kept talking, saying just enough to let her keep going and occasionally nudging her to continue.

I had no idea how much time had passed. Exhausted from crying, Rit leaned limply against me.

"…"

"We'll put together a concrete plan by the day after tomorrow, but we intend to break through the siege and go call for reinforcements. We're going to go through the bewitching woods."

"The bewitching woods?"

"Normally, it would be impossible to get through there, but we're in luck. A high elf named Yarandrala whom we've adventured with before is in a village nearby. They're still fighting the demon lord's army there, so I'd guess Yarandrala has probably taken command of their defensive forces. Her blessing allows her to communicate with plants, and she can make it through that dangerous forest. We're going to save the village where Yarandrala is, meet up with her, and then travel through the woods."

The demon lord's army wouldn't go all out against some tiny little village. Their forces there were likely to be weaker.

"I'll leave it to you all, then. Even if I don't do anything, I'm sure the Hero will be able to resolve it," Rit responded, hardly roused, with her eyes averted. The determined woman hailed as a hero in her own right was nowhere to be found in that face.

"Maybe. But that way won't lead to the best result."

"Why not? It's best for the Hero to save the day, right? All of you are strong. Much stronger than I am. Wouldn't it go smoother than if I fought?"

"Maybe, but if that happened, it would just end up being another case of the Hero passing by and happening to save the day before leaving again."

"What's the difference?"

"I'm sure Ruti could pass through the bewitching woods, lead reinforcements back here, and defeat the demon lord's army. But if she did, then the victor would just be her and her party. It wouldn't be a victory for Loggervia."

"If reinforcements were to come, we'd be glad to fight, too."

"That's not what I mean. What's important here is whether Loggervia's resolve—their pride—is part of it."

Rit's shoulders trembled slightly, but she was still looking down.

"Rit, please listen to me. This is really important."

"...Okay."

"You need to endure the sadness you're feeling and stand back up. You need to break through the bewitching woods with us, be there to request the reinforcements, and fight the demon lord's army side by side with our party."

"Why?"

"If you don't, this battle will only be remembered in Loggervia as the day the great head of the royal guard was lost. Even if the demon lord's army is pushed back, that bitter memory will leave a scar in this country's heart that will never heal."

"…"

"Rit, I've said it before, but you are my comrade. You are one of the Hero's comrades."

The girl looked up slowly. Her expression now hardened with determination. Her blue eyes, still wet with tears, met my own.

"It would be simple enough for Ruti to force your father to write the letter. But it would be even better if you persuaded him. I want Loggervian determination behind the victory in this battle. Without that, even if the country makes it through this hardship, once the Hero is gone, they won't be willing to fight should the enemy return."

"Because we weren't the ones who won."

"Exactly."

"…I got it," Rit said, nodding.

Tears still stained the young woman's face, but a heroic resolve had returned to her expression.

We rose to leave. The remaining things to discuss were better covered in the council room, not her bedroom. Rit walked ahead of me but suddenly stopped and turned around.

"Gideon…truly, thank you. For coming to this country with the Hero, for meeting me, for being willing to call me a comrade…for saving me… Truly, thank you."

There was a gentle smile on her face.

Chapter 5

- - - - - - - - -

A Ring in Amber

The store was open for business again today.

I was preparing medicine to deliver to Newman tomorrow while Rit was watching the shop. Every once in a while, I could hear exclamations of surprise at Rit's presence, but there had been no particular problems.

"It's just a matter of time before rumors start to spread, though."

Zoltan's strongest adventurer had quit and started working at an apothecary. Once word got out, it would definitely cause some controversy. It would be a lie to say I didn't think that was going to be a pain when Rit first said she wanted to work at the shop, but…I didn't feel that way anymore.

"But still, what else can we do about it?"

Should we tell the other B-rank adventurer, Albert? That would promote him from the number two adventurer in Zoltan to number one, after all. I'd only talked to him once before, though, so we were hardly acquaintances.

In the first place, it wasn't like being an adventurer had any fringe benefits or the like. There wasn't any severance payment or pension, so was there any obligation to keep doing it? Wasn't being an adventurer a free-spirited sort of job? If you decided to be one, you could be. If you decided to quit, couldn't you do that, too?

"Right, right. Whether it causes a fuss has nothing to do with us."

After thinking about it awhile, I convinced myself of that desperate theory and focused on the rest of my work, pushing dealing with the problem to a later date.

*   *   *

It was toward the end of the day, nearing sunset.

The standard in this town was for work to end a bit before dark and for people to head home during the twilight hours. Because of that, shops that expected sales from customers returning home from their own jobs would close just a little bit after sunset. The red-light district opened in the evening and maintained hours well into the night for customers who had called it a day.

Red & Rit's Apothecary operated until sunset; we'd be closing up in about an hour. Rit and I were both sitting at the counter, chatting as we waited for customers.

"Oh yeah, I want to get some mead to drink," Rit said.

"Why all of the sudden?"

"No particular reason; I just had an urge to have a drink was all."

"Ah, that happens. But I don't have any mead."

Mead was an alcohol made using honey. It wasn't a particularly high-class liquor, but it was a bit on the expensive end to be drinking all the time. Generally speaking, a cheap wine for the masses was about one-fourth of a payril—one quarter payril coin—per bottle. Whereas mead was two payril per bottle, eight times more expensive. Incidentally, one cup of coffee was one one-hundredth of a payril, a common bronze coin. A four-liter jug of ale or apple wine, lower-class standbys, cost half a payril, which meant fifty commons or two quarter payril.

I had a jug of apple wine and a leather bladder full of a strong alcohol made from tree sap that I had gotten way back as payment when I had taken care of a wounded zoog I ran across in the mountains.

"Mind if I go out to buy some real quick?" Rit asked.

"Sure, just come back before we have to close up," I responded.

"Thanks! Make sure dinner is something that goes with mead."

"Roger. So then bread and something on the heartier side. Snacking on an apple while we drink after dinner would be good, too. We bought groceries yesterday, so that shouldn't be a problem."

I gave her the go-ahead, and Rit leaped from the shop. Literally, not metaphorically. She used the superhuman physical strength she had been granted by her blessing to leap out the door, accompanied by a gust of wind.

"…But why mead all of a sudden?"

And why was she so excited about it? I could feel the time passing idly as I pondered that, when the bell rang as the door opened.

"Wel…come." I unconsciously did a double take, making sure I wasn't seeing things.

"Pretty small setup."

"Good evening," I responded.

The newly minted top adventurer in town, Albert the B Ranker, was standing there with his usual self-important air.

"Um, could I inquire as to the kind of medicine for which you were looking?" I had just decided to make a point of avoiding him, yet here he was, coming to me.

"Hmph, I didn't come to buy medicine."

"…"

I had a feeling this was going to be a pain in the ass. Honestly, I was tempted to tell him to leave if he wasn't going to buy anything. But Albert had a not insignificant amount of influence with the adventurers in town, so if I handled him that curtly, it wouldn't be good for my bottom line down the road. I decided to just hold my tongue.

"…"

"…"

Despite saying he wasn't buying anything, he sure took his time eyeballing the shop. I had no idea what he was trying to do.

"Are you really satisfied with such a meager store?" Albert finally asked.

Oh, so he came to pick a fight?

"I am." I refused to respond to his provocation. I just let it slide with a disinterested response. "My own shop, with customers buying the things I've made, and more than enough income to live a comfortable life with a cute roommate…"

"Roommate?"

Oops, ran my mouth a bit there.

"Ahem. Anyway, I'm satisfied with this shop. I'm not sure what brought you here, but as I clearly don't measure up to your expectations, this is just a waste of your time."

"Happiness is cheap for people who haven't experienced life in the heavens." His barb was filled with sarcasm, but having lived at the level of nobility myself during my tenure as the second-in-command of the Bahamut Knights, that wasn't going to bother me. Propping my head up on my hand, I just fired back with a blatantly disinterested look.

"…Well, whatever. Hey, D rank."

"What, was there something else?"

"I'll ask point-blank. Were you the one who cut down that owlbear last spring?"

"What are you talking about? You were the one who defeated that monster."

Shoot! He had realized that I was the one who had finished off the owlbear. Even in that blazing fire, he had actually noticed the extra wound on it. However highly he thought of himself, he wasn't B rank for nothing.

"The fatal wound on the owlbear was not made by my sword. It was inflicted by a much duller blade… Like that bronze sword of yours, for instance."

"Whoa there. I'm just a D-rank adventurer. There's no way I could cut down a creature that strong." As I spoke, a murderous aura welled up from Albert.

Really? He's seriously going to test me with an attack?

I realized what he was planning immediately but didn't know whether he was actually going to attack with the intent to kill or planning to stop at the last moment.

"I'm going to ask it one more time. You were the one who cut that owlbear, weren't you, Red?"

"I already told you it wasn't me."

Albert kicked off the floor while drawing his sword. He swung the long-sword down toward my collar. The blade stopped right before my neck.

"Whoa?!"

I fell back on my ass a split second later. Albert didn't hide his disappointment as he looked down at me.

"I was going to invite you to join my party, but I guess I was mistaken."

Sheesh, it wasn't easy acting weak and powerless. All of a sudden, a breeze blew through the storefront.

"Ah."

A furious gale collided with Albert's back.

Rit's twin blades slashed at the haughty adventurer. The fact that he was even able to react was to his everlasting credit. But because he caught the attack without being in a proper stance, there was an unsatisfying *plink*, and his sword's blade snapped, severed by Rit's own shotel. Perhaps that had still been enough to kill the attack's momentum, because despite almost toppling over, Albert managed to evade her sword.

Unintentionally, I'm sure, he ended up in a position rather similar to mine when I had purposefully fallen on my butt. But that was all he could do. There was no evading her next attack from that position. And even if he wanted to counter, his sword had been broken.

"Wait, Rit!" I shouted wildly, trying to stop her.

Rit's sword was swiftly brought to a halt. Her lethal gaze and the way her blade was aimed directly at Albert's brow were unchanged, but the girl took a single step back.

"R-Rit?! Why are you here?!"

"Albert, what do you think you're doing? He's precious to me, so depending on your answer, I might just kill you."

"Ah... Gh..."

The man sat beneath the glower of a swordswoman who had fought it out with the demon lord's army. Albert's lips trembled, opening and closing wordlessly.

"He came to invite me to join him. That was apparently a test as part of it."

Rit glared at Albert when I said that. I just shrugged and waved, telling her it was fine. Rit still looked disgruntled as she sheathed her swords.

"Phew."

Just watching was nerve-racking. Albert was reeling as he stood back up. He glanced at the counter where I'd been standing and then turned to face me again, seeing I was standing near the door.

"Why are you there...? When did you...?"

"I didn't want to get caught in Rit's attack."

Albert looked confused, but...

"Get lost," Rit growled menacingly.

"Eep?!" That was enough to set him scurrying out of the shop.

"Red! Are you okay?! You're not hurt, are you?"

"Of course not."

"Good. What was he thinking drawing a sword on you?! You should have just attacked him then and there. It would have been pure self-defense."

"There's no way I could kill the only active B-rank adventurer in Zoltan. He might cause trouble, but he's still critical to Zoltan."

"Really?"

As we spoke, Rit's bloodlust cooled, and her mood shifted back to normal.

"You idiot! Why would you do something so dangerous? You could have at least fought back!" It seemed I was now the target of the girl's anger.

"It was fine. I was pretty confident he would stop at the last second."

"What were you going to do if you were wrong?"

"I'd have fought back."

"How would that even be possible when the blade was practically touching your skin already? ...Can you actually do something like that?"

"Who knows," I said, brushing it off.

I moved on to more important matters.

"You didn't have to toss the mead you went to the trouble to go buy," I chided, holding up the bladder of mead I had caught.

"S-sorry, I just...," Rit stammered, blushing.

"It's fine. Thank you. If anything, I'm happy you got so angry for my sake."

The reason I had leaped from the counter was to catch the mead that Rit had flung aside. Maybe it was a little silly showing off a bit of my speed over something like alcohol after trying so hard to hide my actual strength from Albert, but…it was something Rit really wanted. Her not having it just because of me didn't sit right in my stomach.

"All right, it's a bit early, but how about we close up shop? After we check the books, let's have dinner. Since you got something special, let's relax and drink tonight."

"…Yeah!"

I had a feeling this was going to end up being annoying later, but for now, I wanted to enjoy the present. It would've been a waste when things did get troublesome to not have enjoyed ourselves while we could.

✻   ✻   ✻

Why mead, though…?

It was quite a while later when I finally asked Rit, but apparently, there was a tradition in Loggervia for newlyweds to take one month off work and drink mead while enjoying their honeymoon. Rit had suddenly remembered that and gotten an urge to drink mead with me… At least, that's what she told me.

Of course, when she said that, both our faces reddened.

✻   ✻   ✻

It had been three days since Rit had kicked Albert out of the store. Today was the shop's regular day off, so the two of us went out.

Three men were wearing towels in a stone room, sweat dripping from every inch of our bodies.

The gaze of Gonz, the half-elf, was fixed on the ground below him, staring at the sweat dripping from his face to the towel beneath his feat.

Stormthunder, the half-orc, was enduring it stone-faced with arms crossed.

I was pondering what I could do to get out of this pointless battle of wills and hoping someone would put an end to it soon.

"Haaaaah," Stormthunder said, breathing out slowly.

Oh, can this be done now?

"My body's finally starting to get a bit warm," he boasted, grinning a toothy smile.

We're not really having a competition here!

"Heh, true, it seems like the stove's a bit weak today," Gonz said as he raised his sweat-drenched head with an indomitable smirk.

No, really, though. What are you guys fighting over? Didn't we just come to the public sauna to sweat it out a little? And why are you two staring at me?

"""…"""

What do you expect me to do?

The two men kept staring.

Argh, fine, I get it already.

I stood up and moved toward the stones surrounding the stove. Taking the pitcher of water there, I poured it over the heated rocks. There was a sizzle as steam billowed up. The energy built up in the stones was released and filled the room with a white cloud of heat.

"A bit warmer now?"

""Yeah,"" the two answered.

The three of us grinned at one another.

✳   ✳   ✳

"Geez, Big Brother, this is all because you can't stand losing!" Gonz's little sister, Nao, was dumbfounded as she placed a wet towel on his forehead.

The stubborn carpenter had collapsed from dizziness.

"Heh-heh-heh, I forgot I had a wee bit of a cold today."

But I guess Gonz deserved some credit for his display of the classic blue-collar backbone, still firing back even in such a weakened state.

Stormthunder and I were both at limits of sorts, too, so we were glad for the excuse to get out.

"Sheesh, don't go dyin' in my sauna!" the proprietor complained. Zeff, who ran the steam room, was an old man, getting up there in years.

"And it was such an auspicious day to have Miss Rit come by."

Rit had her hand on her hip as she gulped down some fresh milk.

"Mmm!"

She seemed to be really enjoying it. Maybe I should have gotten some, too.

"Still, there aren't many customers today," Stormthunder murmured as he looked around.

This public sauna was an old one that had been operating for more than sixty years, apparently. There were two rooms: one for men and one for women. Outside the steam rooms was an area to wash the sweat off and clean up when you were done.

Milk, fruit wine, beer, and other drinks were sold outside the sauna. So in addition to cooling off in the washing area, you could also enjoy some drinking.

The people of Avalon love their baths and steam rooms. There weren't many people with proper bathrooms in their homes, but there were many with little sauna rooms. In subtropical Zoltan, getting hot and sweaty in the sauna and then refreshing yourself with a cool water rinse was the way to make it through the summer. Folk still readily took steams in the winter months, too.

This sauna was run by the owner and a young man who helped out part-time. The two of them took care of everything from cleaning the rooms to selling the drinks and maintaining the stoves.

"Are you going to be okay, Gramps?" Stormthunder asked.

"We're all gettin' older," Zeff said with a shrug.

The reason traffic here had gone down was because of the new public bath that had just opened. It had been built by nobles who loved their Central trends. The structure contained both a bath and a sauna. The sauna was not the standard stove style used in Zoltan but instead was a large facility with a heat source underneath the floor to boil water and warm the entire room with steam. Because of that, an entirely new channel had had to be dug from the river, and it wasted a lot of water.

It was a very "noble" sort of setup, being very indulgent. Yet even the working class of Zoltan, who hated Central styles, had taken a liking to its design. You could sweat it out in a hotter and more humid room than Zoltan-style saunas could provide, bathe in cool water as much as you wanted, or even warm up a bit in a heated bath. On top of that, it also had a restaurant, tavern, barbershop, and even a massage parlor. It was an extravagant all-in-one relaxation establishment.

"The competition's just a bit too bad a fit," Zeff said with a tone of surrender.

"*Public baths are places where aristocrats and townspeople alike strip away their clothes and their privilege and can debate one another as individuals.*" Wasn't there a king some two hundred years ago who'd said that? In line with that belief, the new Central-style public bath had been established near the line between the central part of town and the blue-collar part district. Thanks to that, the public saunas and baths on the working-class side of town were quickly losing business.

"Come on! Don't give up without at least fighting back! No one knows what might happen yet!" Nao chimed in from the side.

Oh yeah, hadn't she said she had been coming here since she was young? She probably felt more strongly about it than others who'd moved here later in life, like Stormthunder and me. Zeff's response was anything but motivated, however.

"I can't make a place as big as that. I can barely afford to pay one part-timer. I'm sure they've got a dozen or more full-time employees. Not that I've tried to count."

Nao stomped her foot in frustration. She clearly understood Zeff's point, even if she didn't like it.

"…Ugh, come onnnn! As long as you're open, I'll keep coming here. And I'll get a drink, too! One beer, please!"

"Sure thing," Zeff said with a wry smile as he filled a mug to the brim with the amber liquid.

Stormthunder, Rit, and I were surprised by Nao's outburst, but her deep affection for this place was clear as day.

"I'll keep coming, too," I declared.

"Me, too! I'll come to warm up with Red," Rit added.

Stormthunder and Gonz both nodded.

"Y'all have some strange tastes," Zeff said, waving us off a bit as a smile crossed his wrinkled face.

"This is kind of nice," Rit said with a lonely but happy sort of expression.

I'd only lived in Zoltan for a year, and Rit had only been here about two years, but that moment was somehow a bit emotional for us. We felt attached.

"Hmm."

I started to wonder whether there was something an apothecary like me could do. Not that I was going to think of some brilliant idea on the spot.

Everyone went home satisfied that day after a nice sauna.

✳   ✳   ✳

"Hey, old man, we're back."

"Oh, Red, Nao, and Miss Rit? I was just closing up for the day, but…"

Wait, Rit got "Miss," but Nao and I don't get anything? Well, I guess it's not surprising; Rit was Zoltan's top adventurer.

"What's that bag you've got?" Zeff's sharp eyes glanced at the cloth bag I was holding. "It's got some kinda nice smell to it."

"No surprise you noticed it immediately. I came to see about maybe trying this out."

After the talk at the sauna the other day, Nao had come to my shop, and we'd talked over dinner about how to keep Zeff's business running. Rit had joined in, and we'd all ended up agreeing that it needed something the nobles' big bath didn't have. Figuring out what that something was should've been difficult, but while we were talking, I remembered the smoke therapy that the wild elves used.

The wild elves were said to be the descendants of the ancient elves destroyed long ago. They cast aside the trappings of civilization and lived a primitive life in secluded valleys. No comforts of modern society also meant they didn't have clothes. They were totally naked. They were undoubtedly hardier than humans, but living in a wild valley without clothes or proper tools was difficult. Like anyone else, they got sick at times. When that happened, the wild elves used smoke therapy to treat their illnesses.

They would borrow a cave used by bears to hibernate, cook a soup of various medicinal herbs in a clay pot, and then use the steam from that to warm and heal their bodies.

The scented sachet I was holding was something I had made with the intent of adapting something similar for use in a Zoltan sauna.

"I put some herbs in this, so if you string it up over the stove, the steam should waft up and fill the sauna with the aroma. And it's good for soothing your throat."

The effect itself was kind of, well, I hadn't been able to prepare anything with a particularly special effect on the spot, but the fragrance was nice, and I had chosen a mixture that should've had a relaxing effect.

"How about it? If it works out, I can make more of these sachets and deliver them on a regular basis for you."

"That's something I've never heard of before, all right, but is it really gonna go that smoothly?"

"That's what I wanted to test."

We didn't have a sauna room of our own to test it in. We had at least tried steaming it over a boiling pot at Nao's house to make sure the scent worked, but without actually testing it in a sauna, it was hard to really judge.

"Huuuh, y'all sure do have some odd tastes. You really think this is a problem a bunch of greenhorns are gonna solve?" Zeff asked.

Despite his words, he had a bit of a pleased smile.

"Well, since you went to all that trouble, I guess I can let you give it a try."

✳   ✳   ✳

"This ain't half bad," Zeff admitted in surprise.

"I guess the fragrance is a lot more prominent inside a sauna. This worked better than expected."

The sachet was hanging above the stove, and after adding some water to the stones a few times to create puffs of steam, a pleasant aroma filled the sauna. Even I had been surprised. It smelled much nicer than I'd first thought it would.

"Saunas are an amazing thing. I've been running one since I don't know how long, but there are still things I don't know. To think it could be filled with such a nice smell."

"So? With this, you can still keep your place going, right?" Nao asked with a mixture of hope and fear that this might still not be enough.

Her question made Zeff laugh out loud. His eyes narrowed, and his shoulders shuddered as he guffawed.

"Yeah, I suppose with something like this, I might get a few more customers willing to come. They can't do this at that big ole sauna... I was actin' like I knew it all about the business, but look at me now. Guess I was a bit too quick to give up on running this place."

Zeff had run a public sauna for so many years, he probably thought he knew more than anyone else about it. Every time I had come here, he'd always made tiny adjustments to the stove or the layout of the stones to best suit the outside temperature and weather. Doubtless, he imagined that he had reached the pinnacle of operating a steam room. That was likely why he'd seemed so quick to call it quits.

"It's been awhile since I've been put in my place like this. You've got my thanks, Red, Nao, Miss Rit," Zeff said, beaming.

But that meant there was still more that he didn't know. For Zeff, that was both frustrating and gratifying. At least, that's how it looked to me.

"I want to buy some of those scented sachets, Red. I'm thinking of keeping this shop going a bit longer."

"Hooray!" Nao cheered.

She leaped with joy and hugged Rit with a wide smile, ecstatic at being able to save the place she had been frequenting since she was a child.

"Thanks for you patronage," I said, equally pleased.

The next time I went to the mountains, I made sure to get lots of fragrant herbs.

*   *   *

"Aaah."

I was sitting on a towel, enjoying the sauna while a pleasant fragrance filled the air. Zeff had said to go ahead and hop in, since we had gone out of our way to stop by.

"This was a fantastic idea, if I do say so myself. A sauna revolution."

I allowed myself a little self-congratulation, since I was alone. Getting to relax and take my time in a sauna after-hours wasn't bad, either. Zeff had said not to worry about the time, so I figured maybe I'd even do three cycles.

Suddenly, there came a creak, and the thick door to the sauna opened.

"Waaaah, it really is a lovely fragrance."

"It sure is! This will bring in customers for sure."

Rit and Nao entered.

"W-wait! Why are you two coming in?!"

I frantically wrapped a towel around my waist. The two of them had towels wrapped around their own bodies, but their chests looked ready to burst out from behind the fabric. Rit's weren't exactly small, but Nao's were *big*.

"It's not fair if you get to have all the fun!"

"Yeah!"

"So you decided to come in naked?"

There were places where it was normal to have mixed bathing, but around here, it was standard to have separate baths. Plus, in places that did have mixed bathing, it was normal to wear a swimsuit.

"It's fine. You're the only other person here."

"Wait, wait, wait. It's definitely not fine. Aren't you married, Nao?"

Being in a sauna together with Nao like this, I was going to have to apologize to her husband, Mido. Nao just stared at me blankly.

"Wh-what's with that reaction?" I asked.

"Ah-ha-ha! I've got a towel on; it's fiiine!" She laughed heartily as she put her hands on the portion of fabric covering her waist.

"Okay, okay! I'll get out for now!" I insisted.

It was a shame to have to leave the sauna and its relaxing fragrance, but there was no helping it.

As I tried to leave, however, Rit blocked my way with arms outspread to stop me.

"Wh-why are you…?"

"I-it's fine. Let's just enjoy it together," Rit said as she glanced away a bit, face bright red.

"Should you really be making a cute girl say that?" A suggestive grin crossed Nao's graceful elven face. "If you're a man, just take it like one."

"Gh."

I had a feeling what Nao was saying was probably right. Rit was clearly embarrassed. Her face was bright red. As a man, trying to run away after she had pushed herself that far would just be pathetic.

Thoughts running wild in my mind, I awkwardly sat back down. Rit followed me with a surprisingly meek sort of appearance, sitting right next to me on my left.

"Ah-ha-ha, what are you, a couple of teenagers? What are you getting so embarrassed about?" Nao laughed in amusement.

She sat down a little farther than Rit had. The way she chuckled as she watched us was like the quintessential working-class resident.

"But I suppose it's no surprise you could tell," Nao said to Rit.

"How so?"

"You've got a good eye to pick Red. He's a good man. Way better than any of those snobs in the central part of town."

"Eh-heh-heh." Rit giggled happily.

Having people talk about me like that while I was still sitting there was unbearable. I could feel my cheeks flushing, but I was hoping we could just write it off as the work of the sauna and leave it at that.

"Red saved my son's life. There are some folk who think of him as no more than an eternal D rank, but when it comes to getting medicinal plants, he's a pro who does his job perfectly."

"Yeah, yeah. Red's been that kind of person ever since I first met him. Coming to Zoltan hasn't changed that side of him."

Though wearing so little, the two seemed to be enjoying themselves, talking about me amid the steam of the sauna. Rit even reminisced about things from when we'd been together in Loggervia, too. The two women had really only just met the other day—and through my own doing no less—but they seemed to be good friends already. I'm sure it came from that night we'd been discussing how to keep this sauna from going under.

"Red." Rit glanced over at me.

I did a double take noticing the glistening sweat on her shoulder.

"Let's all come together again sometime," she said with a sparkling smile.

Because of the new experiment with fragrances, this sauna became the talk of the blue-collar neighborhood, and it started drawing lots of customers again, flourishing as it had in the past. For my shop, the contract to supply the bags on a regular schedule was fairly good for business, too. What's more, it was satisfying seeing Nao and her family chatting so happily as they came back from the steam room. It was reminiscent of the sense of accomplishment I had back when I was in the Hero's party and we saved a village.

It had been a day since we signed the deal with Zeff for the scented sachets.

I was getting things in order to open the shop when I noticed a bit of a ruckus outside. When I went out, I saw a bigwig from the Adventurers Guild, a few others from various Merchants and Craftsmen guilds, a government official, aristocrats, and others all lined up in front of the store with grim looks.

"Ah... I suppose you're probably not here looking for medicine."

Every one of them was wearing clothes made of quality fabric with ornate embroidery. Even on a low-end estimate, the cheapest of them couldn't have cost less than fifty payril. They glanced at one another. Galatine from the Adventurers Guild, a big guy at almost two meters tall, stepped forward as the silently elected representative of their group.

"Red, there's something we wanted to ask. Is it true that Rit...the former B-rank adventurer, is living in your house?"

The top brass of Zoltan had finally come to call about Rit.

"It's true. I'm living with Rit, and she's helping me out with my shop."

A murmur ran through the group of men who formed the nucleus of Zoltan.

"We'd like to speak with her...," Galatine said.

"I don't mind, but you caught us in the middle of getting ready to open the shop. Rit's currently double-checking the inventory. If you could wait until she's done with that—"

"Wh-what did you say?! You would have *us* wait?!" someone shouted from the group.

"Rit is an employee here, and she's taking care of an important job right now. If it's something critical like people's lives at stake, then that's another story, but this isn't something that will be hurt by waiting just thirty minutes."

"Is that really for you to decide? Don't you think you should at least talk to Rit first and see if she thinks this is really something that should wait?" Galantine prodded.

"I know her well enough to be able to answer in her place."

"...That's quite the confidence you've got, Red. I didn't know you had that sort of a side to you."

"I'm honestly surprised you know so much about a mere D-rank adventurer."

"I've memorized the faces and records of every adventurer we have on record," Galantine said without a change in expression. His cool gaze as he looked down at me would probably have been enough to make a normal adventurer tremble.

He had been in the previous generation's B-rank party. He was past his prime now, but the pressure he could bring to bear was still there. Not that it meant much to someone like me, who'd been in a party with people who had even more frightening expressions. Danan was like a wild beast in the arenas.

After glaring at me for a minute, Galatine looked almost impressed.

"...Okay, got it. We'll wait a little bit," he said, letting up.

"Thank you for your patience."

There were still complaints, but I just headed back into the shop, putting an end to the conversation. About twenty minutes later, Rit came back from the storage room with a basket full of the medicines to restock the shop front.

"Thank you. I'll take care of setting them out," I said.

"It's fine; I can finish it. The higher-ups are here, right? I think I'll keep them waiting a bit," she said, sticking out her tongue.

I managed a wry chuckle and then turned my attention to ensuring there was enough money to make change at the counter. Yep, there were enough commons, quarter payril, and payril.

"All right, I'm done here. I'll just go turn them down and be right back. I work here now," Rit said.

"All right. I don't know what I'd do without you, so make it quick."

She grinned happily at me, and then, as she headed outside, a smaller, thin man slipped in behind her. He had been standing out front a bit earlier.

"If I recall, you're with the Thieves Guild," I said.

"You're awfully knowledgeable for a D ranker," the thin man responded.

At a glance, the slim man might have seemed like a trivial low-level sort of person, but the way he carried himself and the way his eyes focused on the arms and legs of the person he was dealing with without meeting their eyes had all the hallmarks of a ferocious and skilled coward who constantly lived with the risk of being betrayed.

The Thieves Guild was an organization that operated on the underbelly of society. In other places, they were sometimes called the mafia or a gang. In the East, I believe they were sometimes called yakuza. They were a criminal organization but had established a place for themselves as members of the political establishment under the guise of keeping pickpockets and burglars from doing as they pleased. Not that I had really put much thought into question of whether they were a necessary evil or just plain evil.

It was not that uncommon for the Thieves Guild to approach the Adventurers Guild with a contract, and they had probably approached Rit with a job to take care of some problem or another at some point. As a general rule, though, the Thieves Guild used Albert for their higher-difficulty quests. It was well-known that Albert was close with Golga, the head of the guild.

"Apparently, the others are planning to try to persuade Rit, but she's a true-blue hero. She can already get anything she wants. There's no way they or I could provide the sort of compensation she might want to change her mind. So talking to her is just a waste of time."

And what might she want? What exactly did this guy even know about her?

"So then me?" I asked.

The thief's lips cracked into a broad grin as he took out a small locked box from his cloak and opened it in front of me. Inside was a single elven coin made of pure elven platinum, sitting atop red silk. An elven coin was the most valuable currency on the continent, equivalent to ten thousand payril. The metal it was made of was created back in the ancient time of the elves. It was a long-lost forging method, which meant that not only could it not be counterfeited, it could not even be properly cast.

It was harder than steel and resistant to heat, acid, and corrosion.

On top of that, if you held elven platinum in your hand while connecting with your blessing, in exchange for the metal transforming to worthless lead, it would have the effect of boosting all your blessing's skills up one level for a single minute.

Naturally, it was not a common item or even something to be used in trades between merchants. It was used for exchanges at a national level and would probably be better classified as a treasure than a currency. Although, when I was traveling with Ruti and the others, we didn't hesitate to use them for an advantage in fights against powerful enemies... Well, everyone other than me, of course. All I could use were common skills, so even if they went up a level, it wouldn't have made that much of a difference.

Anyway, it had been a long time since I had seen one of these coins, but it wasn't as if the material was that rare. If you explored deep into ancient elf ruins, you could find a decent amount of it. Not many parties could do that, though.

Even a mainstay in the Thieves Guild probably couldn't have imagined that I had seen more than my fair share of elven coins. Mistaking my expression for shock, he continued, speaking with a proud tone.

"It's perfectly reasonable to be surprised. This is a miraculous item that a man might go his whole life without ever seeing. This is an elven coin. I'm sure you've at least heard of them before, right?"

"Yes, I know of them."

"Then we can make this quick. Will you wash your hands of Rit in exchange for this? With this much money, you could live comfortably for the rest of your life without having to work away at this little shop, right? The world would be better off with Rit adventuring, and she would be better off, too. You'd be happy; Rit would be happy; we'd all be happy, too. Everyone wins. And if you are looking for a woman, I can provide that for you. A looker who can send chills up your spine with a single touch. Can you imagine it? I'm talking a fifty-payril-a-night sort of woman. Not those half-circle quarter payril, either—fifty full payril."

The thief had probably done plenty of touting in the red-light district during his time at the bottom of the ladder. He had so naturally slipped into a clear and fluid sales pitch.

But...

"That's too little."

"Huh?"

"Rit's worth far more than that. Pile up a thousand elven coins, and it still wouldn't be enough."

"What are you saying...?"

"Besides," I said, lowering my voice so Rit, with her abnormally sharp ears, wouldn't be able to hear me. "Rit's infinitely better than any fifty-payril-a-night woman."

The thin man probably sensed that there wasn't any opening there to latch on to. He scoffed slightly as he locked the box and put it back in his cloak.

"Not the least bit moved by ten thousand payril... Are you that big a heavyweight or simply that stupid a fool?"

"I just know she's worth more than that. Why else would the Thieves Guild be willing to pay me ten thousand?"

A sour look crossed the slender thief's face.

"As you wish. Sheesh. I guess it's to be expected of the man Rit chose, but you've got some serious guts for a D ranker. Well, if you ever change your mind, let me know. I'm open to negotiations."

"That won't be necessary, so you can just give up on it."

Still determined, he placed a business card with his name on it on the counter before slipping out of the shop.

From the clamor outside, it was clear that, despite Rit's firm rejection, the top brass refused to give in.

"Is it a problem with the rewards?"

"No!"

"We can arrange ampler compensation."

"I don't need it!"

"We can offer a peerage."

"I refuse!"

"If you want a man, my son—"

""What are you saying?!""

That last comment got shot down by the people around the one who'd made the suggestion, and the man backed off dejectedly.

"Argh, get a grip already!" Rit shouted, finally unable to take it anymore. "I signed a lifetime employment contract for working with Red here! I'm retired from adventuring! And if you try to run Red out of town or anything, I'll be leaving with him!"

Lifelong employment? Someone must have intimated that something might happen to my shop to make Rit snap like that. The blond girl's words transformed our vague arrangement into a more formal, tangible shape I hadn't really considered, and finally, the Zoltan higher-ups gave up and left.

Rit was still indignant as she returned. When she saw my face, she looked embarrassed.

"Did you hear that?" she asked.

"Well, if you shout that loudly..."

"...I was, um, annoyed? They were just so persistent and kept saying such weird things, so I just..."

I waved Rit over. She approached, looking a little uneasy. I gently extended my right hand.

"Hold out your hand," I said.

"?"

When Rit put her hand forward as I'd asked, I wrapped it in both of mine.

"R-Red?"

"It's a present."

I slipped the gift I'd been planning to give her on her first payday into her palm.

"Wha...?"

"It's a bit cheap for you, but call it a deposit on that lifetime employment contract."

"Ah! An amber bracelet!"

Rit held a bracelet with a leather band and a single bead of amber. It was not expensive by any stretch, even for the most modest of adventurers, but...

"This is..."

Rit peered at the yellow-colored bead. Amber was a precious stone made of petrified tree sap. Because it was originally a liquid, it was possible to have tree bark or petals trapped inside. The amber I had given Rit had a leaf in the shape of a ring enclosed within.

"A deposit, huh...?" Rit was smiling as she jokingly held the amber bracelet up to the ring finger of her left hand. "Giving me this might really foster the wrong idea, you know."

Likely getting embarrassed after having said that, Rit covered her mouth with the bandanna around her neck.

"The wrong idea? Then while you've still got the wrong idea, there's something I wanted to buy... Could you tell me what kind of gemstone you'd like?"

Argh, dammit, I was blushing too much. This was just as embarrassing for me as it was for her.

"...Anything is fine. I'd love anything you picked for me."

Unfortunately, blessings couldn't provide any kind of skills when it came to love. Even swordsmen like us, forged in the flames of a hundred battles, could only fall back on inexperienced mumbles... Even so, this moment was precious to me.

Chapter 6

- - - - - - - - -

Fire Mage Dir's Scheme

▸ ▴ ▲ ◂ ◂

Approximately two years ago, in the Duchy of Loggervia.

Rit the hero, Princess Rizlet of Loggervia, rose back up. She had managed to persuade her father, the king, to write a letter requesting aid from the surrounding countries in exchange for relinquishing claims to various watering holes and quarries. The official statement would solicit reinforcements from two neighboring countries, the Duchy of Sunland and the Republic of Beryllia.

Sunland lay on the other side of the bewitching woods. Receiving reinforcements from them in particular would be decisive in determining the outcome of the battle. As was perhaps standard for neighboring countries, Loggervia and Sunland had a history of disputes before the demon lord's invasion had even begun. In fact, the two countries were openly hostile, and Beryllia supported Sunland's claim and, as such, had been on poor terms with Loggervia. But in order to save Loggervia, it was essential to get help from both of them.

The final war council over, I was mentally exhausted. I walked down the hall as I tried to stretch my stiff shoulders.

"Big Brother."

A voice stopped me in my tracks. It was the blue-haired Hero, looking up at me with the same quiet expression she always did.

"Hey, Ruti. The meeting's over. In the end, they went along with all our suggestions. I imagine we'll be heading out tomorrow morning."

"Okay." Ruti nodded but seemed a little sullen.

"Is something wrong?"

"Not really."

"You seem a bit annoyed."

She probably intended to be expressionless, but there was a slight tension to her lips, betraying a touch of melancholy. I had been with Ruti since she was little, so I noticed things like that. Everyone else thought she was antisocial and expressionless, but on the inside, she actually had a pretty wide range of emotions.

"You're getting along well with Rit."

"Hmm? I suppose? She's the sort of person you can't just leave be, I guess?"

"Is that so…?" Ruti's eyes narrowed the tiniest fraction as she glowered at me.

"Ah, I'm sorry. But since she, Ares, and I are dealing with the diplomatic relations, it can't really be helped."

Situations like this were sort of a specialty for me thanks to my training as a knight. Ares had been a high-level government official before joining the party, so he was well qualified, too. Well actually, Ares did know the etiquette and how to compose diplomatic documents, but he didn't really have any sense of diplomacy itself. Perhaps because of the impulse of the Sage blessing, even if what he wanted was to be done, he just couldn't let someone else get the credit for it. His clear self-assuredness that he was the smartest person in the room and his bad habit of looking down on everyone else inevitably reared their heads in those sorts of situations.

But Danan, a martial artist through and through, was out of the question, Theodora the Crusader was an archetypical military sort, too, and Ruti wasn't a skilled orator. She would just end up using the effects of the Hero's charisma to make the other side agree.

It wasn't like I was particularly adroit at negotiations when I was a knight, but Ares and I still ended up being the most qualified for the job. It was a bit of a poor showing, honestly, considering this was humanity's strongest party.

"But Ares is slacking off."

"Well, yeah."

Once a vague course of action had been settled, Ares stopped coming to the meetings. He was laying the groundwork with the nobility of the country by arranging a small-scale get together every night, apparently, though he was probably going to enjoy the inevitable fawning over him, too. He liked that sort of thing.

"The three of you are talking late into the night, but if Ares isn't there…then it's just the two of you," Ruti said with a look of dissatisfaction before tapping my chest. "I want you to be with me today."

"Okay, I get it, I get it. Why don't we get ready for tomorrow together, then?"

Hearing that, Ruti finally looked satisfied and nodded with a quiet expression.

✳   ✳   ✳

True to the plan, the first thing we did was scatter the demon lord's forces attacking the forest village. The lower-tier demons making up the infantry of the force there withdrew without too much resistance.

"Gideon! You finally came!" a long-eared high elf exclaimed as she wrapped me in a powerful hug.

"I'm glad to see you in such good spirits, Yarandrala. Sorry for being late."

"It's fine. They weren't serious about attacking this village anyway. The hug was just because I was happy to see you!"

Yarandrala beamed gallantly as she kept her arm clamped around my waist. She was close enough that our cheeks were almost rubbing together.

Generally, high elves kept a distance from others until they made friends, but once they did, they apparently enjoyed a physical sort of intimacy. It wasn't particularly related to love or anything, but even knowing that, a human like me still got a bit flustered by it. It seemed high elves found it amusing when humans they got along with became embarrassed, which just aroused their affection even more.

"Gideon, who is she?" Rit asked, shocked by the high elf who suddenly engulfed me in a hug when we reunited.

"Ah, this is Yarandrala, a high elf. She's the one who can help us get through the bewitching woods."

She was the other crux of this plan. The bewitching woods along the border of Loggervia was the dangerous forest that the wood elves around here had chosen as the location of their final stand back in the era of the previous demon lord. They had cast countless layers of magic to transform it into an inescapable and unexplored region. It was unknown exactly what had become of those elves who had fought here, but it was a fact that the bewitching woods had swallowed up dozens of skilled adventurers.

"I have a blessing that allows me to communicate with plants and borrow their strength," Yarandrala said proudly as she looked at Rit. The power to speak with plants was one of the benefits of the elf's blessing of the Singer of the Trees.

"The magic placed on the bewitching woods has no effect on beings born in the woods, so by talking to the plants, it is possible to learn the correct way through."

With Yarandrala, we could make it through the bewitching woods. The perimeter the enemy had formed was thinner near the deadly forest, and they would be completely defenseless once we crossed. The members of our expedition were Ruti, Rit, Yarandrala, Ares, and myself. With the five us, the odds of success were high.

Glancing around, Ares was conspicuously absent. After searching a bit, he appeared to be spurring on a man who was the head of a mercenary band. It was a rare sight, since Ares usually didn't pay much heed to soldiers' morale.

*   *   *

"All right, I leave the rest to you," Ares said to the man wearing a hat-style helmet with a wide brim called a kettle hat.

"Aye, sir. I'll be sure that the residents get there safe. And you can count on me for defense, too!" the man said, bowing his head.

The kettle-hat man was named Dir. He was a mercenary, hired by Loggervian aristocrats, who had served as an intermediary between Ares and the aristocrats and had helped out with gathering mercenaries.

The force of fifty or so sellswords had officially been gathered by Ares. His role in the upcoming fight was to go with the group headed out to call for reinforcements, but he had arranged to have a mercenary force under his name in order to be able to claim that he had helped with the defense of the battle as well. Money earned by the Hero's party was only to be used for dealing with the demon lord, not for personal glory. However, Dir had approached Ares with such flattery and assembled more than fifty mercenaries without any payment.

Their efforts and accomplishments would be credited to Ares, and pleased by that fact, rather unlike himself, Ares went out of his way to offer encouragement to them, even going so far as to cast some modest support spells and the like on them.

"But to cross the bewitching woods and solicit reinforcements, I'm in awe of your bravery, sir."

"Thanks to you, we were able to gather information necessary for the trip. Just between us, Gideon was the one who came up with this plan. He has a fondness for gambles with low chances of success, so I always have to follow behind to clean up after him."

Ares had asked Dir about any dangers lurking within the bewitching woods that had made the rounds among the nobles. How much faith could actually be put into the rumors passed around by wealthy men who had never ventured farther than their own estates, though? For Dir, the truth didn't matter. As long as his reports sounded believable, it was fine.

"I thank you for your faith in me, sir. And the decisiveness to act on it is to be expected of the great Sage."

Ares happily accepted the praise, more pleased than he had ever been. Dir's face was hidden in the shadow of the kettle hat as he lowered his head, careful that neither Gideon nor Rit could see it.

If they could have seen his face, they might've recognized the man glaring sidelong at Rit as the fire mage the blond princess had run out of that town.

✳   ✳   ✳

"Haaaaah." Rit sighed.

In the bewitching woods, the voices of the spirits she should have been able to sense because of her Spirit Scout blessing could not reach her. The illusionary magic confused even them. Partly because of that, Rit could not even tell whether their group was actually advancing through the woods. Her sense of direction and the passage of time seemed to have vanished. All the young woman could do was suffer, stewing in her unease and impatience.

And...

Glancing over, she saw the beautiful high elf chatting intimately with Gideon. Her chest tightened at the sight. She felt stupid for having spent so much time with him in Loggervia.

Gideon was one of the Hero's comrades. He was a true hero, who would lend a helping hand to anyone in need. Of course, the young man tried to encourage her when she was depressed, and of course, he would do his best to save the princess's home.

How long had it been since she had stopped being able to look him in the eye? When she spoke with Gideon, she'd often end up smiling or blushing. To hide it, Rit had taken to covering her mouth with a bandanna. Something about it was just so embarrassing. To hide the feeling, she began speaking more harshly.

Just yesterday, when they had been talking about Loggervia, the topic had shifted to how Gideon would have run the country, and even though they had just been making idle conversation at first, she ended up yelling at him, saying "It's not like I want you to stay behind in Log-gervia! Don't get the wrong idea!"

Gideon looked flabbergasted after that outburst, and Rit regretted it from the moment the words crossed her lips. She had not meant it to be like that, but for some reason, she'd lost the ability to have a proper conversation with Gideon. She'd averted her eyes from him, her face red.

"…"

And in avoiding him, she met the gaze of Ruti, who stared coolly at Rit. The princess had buried herself in her sleeping bag to escape and closed her eyes.

The next day, she had intended to apologize to him, but for some reason, he was smiling at her warmly, and the young adventurer felt she'd missed her chance to broach the topic.

She'd been like that ever since they had set out. Compared to Yarandrala, who was walking beside Gideon and chatted so easily with him, or Ruti, who, despite her expressionless demeanor, still managed to demonstrate a deep affection for Gideon in everything she did, Rit was just spinning her wheels.

"What am I doing?"

Struck by a sense of self-loathing, Rit hung her head as she walked at the tail end of the party. According to Yarandrala, they would exit the forest tomorrow. Rit had subconsciously complained about how everything looked the same a few times, but Gideon had tried to cheer her up.

Did I ever properly thank him after that?

Rit was feeling increasingly depressed.

"Hey."

"Hmm? Oh, Yarandrala. What is it?"

At some point, the elf had started walking next to her. The woman was bent over, peering at Rit's face, which was focused on her feet.

"I asked a white birch tree, and apparently, there's a river a little past here," Yarandrala said. She tugged at Rit's clothes. "Your clothes and body are dirty, so why don't we take a break and go bathe?"

"Huh? Bathe?"

"It'll help pick you up. It's a high elf proverb that cleanliness fulfills the body and mind while evil breeds in impurity."

Rit was the princess of a royal family, so she considered herself someone who kept herself fairly clean, but Yarandrala was on another level. Gideon and the others would diligently set up camp and make sure not to start any fires because it'd upset the plants of the bewitching woods, despite causing their party more difficulty. Yarandrala, however, would shamelessly use a full bucket of water to rinse herself. Rit could not help but admire it. Even she could not bring herself to do that much, so instead, she helped Gideon and the rest of the party. But it was apparently just part of high elf culture to be finicky about cleanliness. Their values were a little different from humans'.

"But—"

"We're going to go ask for reinforcements after this. You looking like that won't be doing us any favors. Let's go. Hey, Gideon! We're going to go wash up a bit, so you all should take a break."

"Eh? I didn't say I was going..."

But when Gideon glanced over at them:

"Yeah, I suppose it's about time for a break," he said with a nod.

"Are you really going to indulge Yarandrala again?!" Ares groused indignantly.

But Gideon just patted the other man's shoulder.

"It's fine, isn't it? And we promised to follow her instructions while we were in the bewitching woods, didn't we?"

"Your softness is the reason that...!"

Gideon was taking the blame for the high elf. When Rit realized this and was about to speak up, Yarandrala just gently shook her head.

"It will be fine. Just leave it to Gideon and let's go."

"But."

Looking over to the young man, he just waved his hand, gesturing for Rit to not worry about it and go ahead. He had a wry smile, as if he felt bad for having made the blond princess worry about him at all. Seeing his expression, giddiness rocked her mind. She could not really understand it herself, but a strong urge to hug Gideon washed over her. If Yarandrala had not taken her by the hand, she might actually have run over and embraced him.

✳   ✳   ✳

The river was a small one. At its deepest point, it barely came up to the waist.

Because it was in a forest entirely untouched by humans, though, the water was totally clear and clean. So clear that Rit was hesitant to submerge her dirty body in it. Yarandrala, however, seemed unperturbed as she immersed her beautiful, naked figure in the river.

"Come in, Rit. It's cool and feels lovely."

"This isn't the season for that."

It was currently autumn. Beneath the forest trees, the climate was strangely warm, to the point that Rit had worked up a sweat after walking for an entire day, but it still wasn't really temperate enough to be playing in a river.

Rit sat down on the riverbank and dipped her feet in its clear water.

"Cold!"

The young woman reflexively pulled her feet back. Then she gradually lowered her legs, enjoying the comfortable coolness as she slowly grew acclimated.

In the end, Rit also stripped and entered the river.

"Phew."

It was cold. There was a calm voice in the back of Rit's mind asking how exactly they were going to warm up after getting out of the water in the bewitching woods where they couldn't build a campfire, but her desire to cool her head was stronger.

"Hey, Rit."

Yarandrala seemed to be freely enjoying herself, swimming uninhibited. Rit had been idly wondering whether high elves were naturally more resistant to cold than humans.

"You like Gideon, don't you?"

"Huh?" Rit suddenly snapped back from her daydreaming. "Wh-why are you asking that all of a sudden?"

"If you could see yourself, you'd know," Yarandrala said, breaking into a laugh.

Rit's face turned red, and she submerged herself under the water.

Yarandrala swam over to Rit.

"You're a wonderful person, and Gideon's pretty taken by you, too."

"...Really?"

"But you should probably work on your habit of getting angry when you're embarrassed."

"Ugh...yeah...," Rit said, mortified.

Whenever Rit got harsher with Gideon, it was generally because it had become obvious she was embarrassed.

"If you're going to try to hide the embarrassment, then just go all out with the affection and play it up a bit. If you're going to get so flustered, at least say something worth getting embarrassed over first."

"Even if you say that...it's not like I can just flip a switch..."

"Really? I'm sure if you express your feelings straightforwardly, Gideon will respond to how you feel."

"What about you, then? You seem to get along well with him... Do you have the same sort of feelings as me?"

"Me? You've got it wrong."

"Really?"

Yarandrala was smiling, but to Rit, her expression conveyed a faint loneliness.

"High elves have a bit of a longer life span than humans. I wouldn't end up loving a human like that. I've learned that the hard way. You could almost say the great tree in the capital is my true love now. I'm the Singer of the Trees, after all."

"..."

"I might not look it, but I'm pretty old, you know? A high elf's appearance doesn't change much, so it can be hard to tell."

"Y-yeah."

"So to me, Gideon is more like a best friend, or a comrade in arms, or even the human I consider most trustworthy. But that isn't love." Having said that, Yarandrala wrapped Rit in a tight hug. She could feel the warmth of the high elf's body. They may have both been women, but they were still both naked. Rit, with her human sense of values, could feel a shyness welling up in her. Yarandrala's serious tone quickly dismissed the girl's feelings, however.

"I want Gideon to be happy. He has always borne all the hard work for his comrades and will probably continue to do so, but I want him to live a bit more for himself. I want him to be able to enjoy a more standard, straightforward sort of happiness living with someone he loves."

"Yarandrala…"

"I can't share Gideon's worries. None of them realize it, but Gideon's strengths lie beyond things like blessings and skills. I can't take his place."

"Yeah, I understand. If he hadn't said what he did…I don't think I would be here now. Because he was there for me, I was able to reach a place where I could try to fight again."

Rit understood the feelings Yarandrala held for Gideon. She felt the same way. It was a deep affection, the sort of feeling one might bear for a precious friend or a sibling. A respect for someone, simply wishing the best for them.

"Gideon is strong. But he isn't invincible. He can be hurt by heartless words, and when he's sad, he cries like anyone else would. Everyone has taken it for granted that they can rely on Gideon, but I think if things continue the way they have, there will be problems."

Rit could not respond. To her, Gideon seemed an even more perfect person than the Hero. On an intellectual level, she could understand what Yarandrala was saying, but it was not really something she could visualize.

But I want to understand.

All she had seen so far was Gideon's strength, the heroic man who always came to save Rit when she was suffering, but that was not all there was to him. He was human, just like her. Their blessings were different, but he was a man who could be hurt just as easily as anyone else.

Yarandrala smiled sweetly at the blond girl's expression.

"I think you and Gideon just might be able to make it work, and you might be able to do more than simply depend on him. You could help support him, too."

"Me...? But I've only ever been supported by him."

"That's fine. Because in the end, you really love him."

"...Yeah, I do. I love him."

"Then it will be fine. When Gideon's suffering, he'll lean on you."

Yarandrala seemed sure of this. Rit was surprised the elf held that sort of opinion of her. It was a bit embarrassing, but the princess also felt much closer to Yarandrala, who cared so much for Gideon.

✳   ✳   ✳

From Rit's perspective, everywhere in the bewitching woods looked the same. No matter how much they walked, it never felt like they were making any progress. It was just day after day of torturous changelessness. However, that finally came to an end, and they made it out of the forest that was said to swallow up all who dared enter.

And what should have greeted them was hope, the lands of the Duchy of Sunland, famed for its bazaars.

The bright vista they should have seen, though, was instead being trampled by a dark horde of orcs.

"Why...?"

Rit sat on the ground, shocked.

The party was hiding in the shade of the trees as they peered out at the scene. The road a short distance beyond the underbrush was filled with horses clad in riveted leather armor. It was a battalion of orc hussars. They were patrolling in shifts, executing careful rounds so as not to miss anyone coming out of the woods.

The party's gambit was dependent on the demon lord's army's belief that the bewitching woods were impassable. It was for that reason that Gideon and Rit had limited the number of people who knew the whole plan to the bare minimum. They had only told the nobles that they would use the abilities of the Hero, a sage, a guide, and Rit to break through the enemy encampment without being noticed.

Gideon had not even scouted the bewitching woods because he did not want it getting out that he'd been in the area. He had merely trusted Yarandrala's word when she said she could make it through the forest and had made no effort at all to corroborate that. He had said as much to Ruti and Ares, explaining why, but…to Ares the Sage, entrusting his life in an unknown place to the word of a comrade he did not know that well was unacceptable. He had subsequently leaked details to the mercenary, Dir, in order to further research the woods.

Rit was in utter despair, and Ares was speechless. Gideon merely faced the reality of the situation. Internally, he wanted to rampage, to scream and shout, but it was not as if doing that would improve their situation. The young man had trained himself in that sort of emotional control.

Besides, having heard Ares talk so much about the bewitching woods during the trip, it was not as if he hadn't considered that something like this might happen. To the extent he had envisioned this possibility, Gideon could have been said to be as calm and collected as Ruti. The Hero herself stood beside her brother and observed the fiendish forces placidly.

"Big Brother, what should we do?" Ruti asked.

There was no fear or panic in her voice. As the Hero, despair was something to move beyond, not to be overwhelmed by. Reassured by his younger sister's tone, Gideon studied the orc hussar troops with the keen eye of a hawk.

"Their forces there are a bit thin. If we were going to break through, that would be the place."

"Yes, I agree. But it would be hard as we are now."

If they were leading a force of one hundred, they would undoubtedly be able to breach the enemy lines. Orc hussars made up the core of the demon lord's army, but they were not well trained and were well-known for retreating when their enemy had the upper hand. Their strength was in flanking attacks and wide-range pillaging, things that took advantage of their mobility.

Indeed, because they were so quick to retreat, they could continue ransacking elsewhere without being wiped out, which made them difficult to deal with. No experienced knights of any country on the continent of Avalon would lose to such creatures in battle. However, because the knights wore heavy armor, they could not catch up to the hussars and truly rout them.

In this situation, all the party needed to do was get past them. It was a much simpler task than wiping them out.

But there were only five of them.

Just five people. Before their meager group was a force of at least two thousand. They would have to defeat several hundred orcs with nothing more than their own power. All while continuing to run. Every one of the five of them had a strength that would never lose in a one-on-one battle. Even against dozens of hussars, none of them would fall. If the five worked together, they could probably even vanquish a hundred, but that was their limit.

There were just too many.

They were each heroes who might one day be so overwhelmingly powerful as to be able to face those sorts of odds, but at that moment, they were still at a level that the five of them together could not match a force of such strength.

"All right, here's my idea," Gideon said, steeling his resolve. "I'll draw away the enemy. Ruti and Rit, while that's happening, I want you to try to break through their line."

The blond princess had still been feeling down, but suddenly looking up at Gideon's face, the young woman appeared as if she was about to cry.

Rit was on a drake borrowed from Sunland and riding hard. Her usual willful attitude was nowhere to be seen.

A bit of a silver lining to the terrible situation in which they had found themselves was that Sunland had been wary of the demon lord forces deployed along the edge of the bewitching woods and had sent their own army along the border. Having broken through the enemy's line, Ruti, Rit, and Ares met up with the Sunland army. The three had requested aid on the spot from Prince Blaze, the commanding officer in the field, and then moved back across the border with a force of Sunland drake knights.

Altogether, there were five hundred of the fearsome soldiers. Both riders and steeds were heavily armored. Following behind was a compliment of two thousand infantrymen, but it had already been more than an hour since Gideon and Yarandrala had drawn the enemy's attention to create an opening for Ruti and Rit's group. Waiting for the infantrymen to catch up would've taken too long.

"I beg of you, Almighty Demis and Larael, guardian of hope, please watch over Gideon. Victy, guardian of martyrs, please don't take Gideon away," Rit prayed as she spurred her drake on.

The force they had secured would surely be enough to save Loggervia. That alone should've been enough for Rit to rejoice. But in that moment, Rit forgot all about her home country and prayed only that Gideon still lived.

Faced with five hundred drake knights charging in formation with spears at the ready, the orcs were swept up in a moment's fearful stir, but upon seeing Ruti and Rit riding at the head of the force, the monsters started jeering loudly.

"Look! The cowardly Hero came back to give us another feather in our cap!" The orcs believed they had just cornered the Hero's party. It was true that Ruti had cut down countless orcs who stood before her in order to pass through their lines. It was also true, though, that the Hero's party had desperately fled to escape the onslaught of sabers that had borne down on them like a storm. The wounds had only been minor, but the orcs' blades had cut their flesh and drank of their blood.

"We've got more soldiers! Surround and crush 'em!"

Using their superior mobility to flank the enemy was the standard maneuver for the hussars. Drake knights would normally be forced to perform a series of hit-and-run-style clashes when facing an enemy that outnumbered them four to one. But in terms of mobility, the orcs—with their lighter armor—were much more agile. The fiends should've been able to take care of the knights and head home with another achievement to boast of before the distant infantry ever arrived.

Rit knew this, of course. She had raced there driven by her concern for Gideon, but she could feel a sense of dread as she saw the dull flashes of the orcish weapons through the cloud of dust.

"Rit," Ruti said as she rode alongside her.

"Wh-what?! I'm not scared!"

Ruti was expressionless as she quietly looked at her flustered blond companion.

"Disperse."

"Eh?"

Ruti suddenly raised her left hand. It was the signal to break away. The knights' commanding officer responded immediately, sounding a bugle. The next instant, the orc forces unleashed a hail of arrows.

"Don't worry, orc hussar bows are diversionary. They're only fired randomly, so they aren't a threat as long as none of us are too bunched up."

Readying their swords, Ruti and Rit cut down any arrows that came their way. They could hear the sound of the metal arrowheads glinting off armor behind them. There were a few cries of pain, but because the knights had properly distanced themselves, the damage they suffered was minimal.

"But at this rate—!"

Their scattering also reduced the strength of their charge. For a cavalry charge, it was best to maintain a dense formation while breaching at a single point in the enemy's formation. A dispersed charge was devoid of any impact or force.

Doubt reared its head in the back of Rit's mind, and she wondered whether it might not have been better to accept a few more losses in order to maintain the formation. Ruti's cool expression remained unchanged, however, as she held the Holy Demon Slayer aloft and urged her drake to run even faster.

"Wh—?! Wait! Charging alone?!"

Ruti moved faster and faster atop her mount. Rit could only assume she must have had some kind of riding skill. The princess turned adventurer tried to keep up, but it was a rate of acceleration she could not match. The lone Hero reached the army of two thousand hussars. Even with a blessing that had reached a level that one could truly call heroic, Ruti needed everything she could muster just to protect herself. At first, Rit assumed it would be a repeat of when she and the Hero had been surrounded by the foul creatures, desperately trying to escape their ranks.

The thought was quickly proven wrong, though, as orcs and their horses suddenly went flying through the air.

"Huh?"

A single swing of Ruti's sword sent five of the hussars flying. Every orc sailing through the air had been cut in half, armor and all. Masses of flesh thudded to the ground. Some of the felled monsters' comrades were knocked down by the corpses or else bucked off their steeds panicked at the gruesome sight before them.

Ruti swung her sword again and again. Every swipe of her blade sent large groups of orcs into the air.

"Wh-wha—? B-bastard! When did you learn to do that?!" one of the orcs screamed, his ferocious face twisted in terror.

"I couldn't make a scene before. I'm serious now."

With the plan for Gideon and Yarandrala to lure the enemy away, Ruti could not afford to fight seriously. Had she stood out, it would've just drawn the orcs after her, rendering the risk those two had taken meaningless. It would have compromised the entire plan.

Three orcs, including the commander of the hussar forces, roared and charged, though they were obviously frightened. However, Ruti just swung her blade at them head-on. The sabers of the orcs were infamous for the swathe of destruction they'd cut across Avalon. Yet they shattered easily, and the bodies of their bearers were left twisted, collapsing to the ground, still clutching the hilts of their severed swords.

One after another, the orcs fell. Even as the drake knights approached, the orcs could not take their eyes off Ruti as she flicked her blade to remove the blood splattered on it. They were unable to look away; they dared not, because the Hero was terrifying. If a man-eating dragon were right next to you, would you really be able to take your eyes off it? Even as the monsters were about to be run through by the spears of the knights, compared to that terrifying Hero, spears were…

The force of the hussars began to weaken. Rit and the Sunland knights finally arrived and charged toward their enemy. The orcs could not even put up a proper resistance, instead collapsing in the face of Rit's swords and the knights' spears. The spirit scout adroitly slashed two orc hussars who rushed her, easily knocking them to the ground. The orc sabers that had seemed so menacing when she'd been fleeing now felt like a scant showing.

"So this is the strength of the Hero…"

Before Rit even realized it, the knights were roaring victoriously, even though they had only just seized control of the first contact. The orcs were already on the verge of a full retreat, and some had even started to run. The rout was just a matter of time.

The key to victory in a battle pitting five hundred versus two thousand had been the lone Hero. The way she had cut into the enemies head-on and her immense martial prowess and charisma caused the enemy to cower and her allies to forget their fear. That was the war fought by the Hero, Ruti.

But Ruti did not even exalt in the victorious cheers of her allies. She just continued fighting detachedly.

*   *   *

"Yo."

In the middle of the battlefield, Yarandrala and Gideon stood battered and bruised but still alive. Gideon continued to look fairly hardy thanks to his Immunity to Fatigue, but Yarandrala appeared exhausted. Her neat high elf face betrayed her overexertion.

After the two of them had pulled off the feint, they had apparently kept the ruse and continued running. They must have stolen some orc horses partway through, too, because there were two mounts that looked quite unhappy snorting next to them.

"I'm only still alive because Yarandrala came with me."

"Me, too. If it wasn't for Gideon, there's no way I would have made it."

They grinned at each other. Their wounds had already been taken care of by healing magic, but their armor was covered in scratches, proof that the two of them had suffered a number of wounds and continued fighting regardless. Gideon's trusted sword, Thunderwaker, was still covered in a thick coating of orc blood.

"Y-you idiot…"

Elated, Rit was about to rush to them, but…a smaller-framed girl cut in even faster from the side.

"Big Brother." Ruti gently touched Gideon's face with both hands. "I'm sorry. There wasn't any other way. Never again."

"It's fine. As you can see, Yarandrala and I are safe."

"Never again," Ruti said with quiet, firm determination.

Ruti was usually so calm, never showing emotion. There had been no exaltation, pity, or even hatred as she killed the orcs, yet now she showed a powerful affection for Gideon, even though her expression did not change.

Neither Rit nor Yarandrala could bring themselves to say anything.

When Gideon had said he would face the orcs himself and lure them away, Rit had been against it, of course. Ares had criticized it as rash, too, but Ruti had reined them in.

"Trust him."

"B-but."

"Yarandrala, I want you to go with him."

"Got it. Leave it to me."

"Wait, Ruti! I can't accept that..."

"I'm giving orders to my comrades. I don't need your consent," Ruti said as she looked Rit in the eye. The Hero did not glare; it was her default expression.

"Ah, uh..."

But Rit had been unable to say anything under the pressure of that gaze. Gideon patted Rit's shoulder as she recoiled.

"It's fine. I don't try to do things I can't do."

Despite the fact that he was the one doing the most dangerous job there, he had gone out of his way to reassure Rit. At the time, in her heart, Rit had been enraged at the thought that the Hero would sacrifice her own brother for the sake of some supposed justice, but she realized now that she had misunderstood.

Seeing the two of them holding each other like that, Rit could not hide her shock.

I never thought Ruti could look like that.

Ruti had actually been more concerned about Gideon than anyone, but there had still been no other way. Because he understood that, Gideon had volunteered to be the diversion. He didn't want Ruti to have to be the one to suggest sending her brother to near-certain death.

"It must be nice," Rit muttered to herself as she looked up at the sky a short distance from the two of them.

In the end, Rit did not join the Hero's party. Gideon seemed disappointed. To the princess, Ruti looked relieved.

Part of the reason she had stayed behind was to help oversee the restoration of Loggervia, but even more so, she had felt it wrong to come between Ruti and Gideon. At least for now. Gideon was still too important to his younger sister.

After the man she loved left, Rit cried by herself for a little while.

*　　　　　　*　　　　　　*

"Tch!"

With his things hastily gathered in a bag, Dir the Fire Mage fled Loggervia looking annoyed.

He had betrayed humanity and sided with the demon lord's army for the promise of money. Realizing the situation had turned against him, he immediately moved out. The man had gotten into the castle under the auspices of the head of the royal guard, Gaius—the transformed Shisandan—and knew he would get caught quickly as soon as the war was over. It was the right time to leave.

"Don't you dare forget this, Rit. I'm a vengeful man. Someday, when you're happiest, I'll appear and destroy everything you love."

There was a hideous hatred in his sinister gaze as he spat on the road and then fled. He kept turning to look back, unable to let go.

✻   ✻   ✻

Present day. Zoltan's slums, Southmarsh.

Southmarsh was home to a conspicuously out of place manor. It was the residence of Bighawk, the number two man of the Thieves Guild. Feared for his brutal methods, the giant of a half-orc had migrated to Zoltan from lands beyond.

A thug known as Dir, who stood before Bighawk, had a menial smile plastered across his gaunt face. The vengeful fire mage readily bowed his head to Bighawk. Dir's stance conveyed extreme obsequiousness toward one more powerful than him, but there was no hint of fear in his manner.

This is nothing compared to dealing with the demon lord's army's Asura demons.

Even after fleeing Loggervia, Dir had continued his life of infamy, working as a mercenary outlaw all around the continent. Along the way, he had been an informant for the demon lord's forces as well. The result was that he'd burned all his bridges and had to flee to Zoltan and the frontier.

"Anyway, what I'd like you to do is take care of the Rit situation."

"I'd be happy to do anything within the limits of my capabilities."

"The Thieves Guild would rather Rit not retire from adventuring. Do you know why that is?"

"Ummm, because they don't want to lose someone to hire for difficult jobs?"

"No."

Bighawk slammed his tree trunk–like leg down on the floor with a thud. Dust fluttered down from the ceiling and sprinkled over Dir's head. The fire mage felt an urge to brush it off but resisted.

"Cases we can't handle ourselves, we can just get Albert's party to take care of. The problem is if someone with interests opposed to our guild contracts Rit the hero."

"Ah."

"She's this country's wild card. Every group with any sort of power in the area would pay a steep price if she stood against them. When she gets involved in something, even the Thieves Guild just sucks it up and backs down."

"So why not celebrate her retirement?"

"Because it's not that simple. In the past, if there was a situation where we absolutely could not afford to have her stand against us, we could just send her an unrelated request to keep her far away from Zoltan while we took care of things. Now, though, she's always going to be in town. What if she goes against us on a whim? It's gonna be bad for business in ways you can't begin to imagine."

"I see."

That was the point that really concerned Bighawk. The wild card they had been able to control to some extent had entirely slipped its leash. And if they tried to pull one of their tried-and-true assassinations, they would be targeting a genuine hero strong enough to have the upper hand in a brawl with the entire Thieves Guild. The Thieves Guild chief and every last one of the higher-ups all agreed that making a move on someone like that would be suicide.

"So we come to you, Dir. You seem to have some kind of dirt on the girl."

"Or something, at least. It might not be enough to get her to do whatever

I say, but it might be enough to at least get her to go back to adventuring or else to push her out of Zoltan," Dir intimated with a sly grin.

It was no coincidence that this man had been summoned by Bighawk. He had been playing dumb before, but knowing that the Thieves Guild was struggling with what to do about Rit retiring, Dir had implied to a member of the organization that he knew something about her past.

"Huuuh. That's quite intriguing. I'd like to hear a bit more, but… you don't really plan on telling, right? Our group's got no intention of taking a stance on Rit one way or the other."

"H-huh?" Dir was flustered at the unexpected turn as he looked up at Bighawk's face.

The half-orc avoided meeting his gaze, grabbing a walnut from a plate nearby and crushing its shell with his thick fingers before tossing the nut into his mouth. He chewed the walnut with an audible crunch. Dir was taken aback as he waited for Bighawk to explain.

"Basically, the gist of it is that I'd be quite happy if this problem just took care of itself."

"!"

Dir nodded, understanding where Bighawk was going.

"And if that problem resolves itself, might I happen to get a nice little something?"

"You'd get nothing at all, since the Thieves Guild has nothing to do with this. Perhaps you might find yourself a nice job carrying baggage shortly afterward or something. Maybe those bags would be filled with money."

So basically, instead of a reward, just "steal" that money. Catching Bighawk's drift, Dir cackled.

"Understood. I'll be taking my leave now, then," he said.

"All right. Sorry for calling you out here. Hey, one of you show him out."

Some rather unpleasant-looking men from the Thieves Guild showed Dir to the door with the utmost courtesy. A little parting gift, a bag of silver coins, had been slipped into his breast pocket.

"I've been rotting away in obscurity to the point of washing up in a piece-of-shit town like this, but looks like my luck's finally about to change."

I'm gonna get to smash Rit's happy little life.

The thought of that made Dir want to cackle, but he forced himself to stay quiet.

✳   ✳   ✳

Maybe it's a bit premature, but I, Rizlet of Loggervia, am currently utterly happy.

I never would have dreamed I would get to live together with Gideon—no, Red—when I left Loggervia.

"Lunch is ready," Red called.

"Okaaay."

Hearing the voice from the kitchen, I hang the ON BREAK sign on the store's door and headed to the living room. My stomach is already preparing to enjoy some more of Red's delicious cooking.

"Today we're having bacon gratin, a seafood soup, and some bread."

The ingredients themselves are not particularly expensive or rare, but his cooking always looks and smells so delicious. Just seeing the grill marks on the bacon gratin is enough to pique my appetite, and the smell of the sea from the soup is irresistible.

"Thank you!"

First, I drink a bit of water to cleanse my palate. Then I take a spoonful of the gratin… Mmmm, the steam has such a delectable smell… Hmm, but it seems a bit hot; maybe starting with the soup was better? It would be a waste if I burned my mouth and couldn't taste the food he made.

The soup has a bit of red fish meat and two shellfish in it. It also has some vegetables—cabbage and little green things. Herbs? The addition of those as a garnish to decorate the amber soup is just superb.

I blow on it a little to cool it, and then the taste of the sea fills my mouth as I hold it there for a moment. But it doesn't have a fishy sort of flavor. Supposedly, boiling the seafood in an alcohol of some kind gets rid of that fishiness. Is this taste from the wine he used for the preparation?

I can't wait; what about the bacon gratin?

The surface is fried to a golden brown, but the inside is pure white and soft. It gives off a rich steam. Thick-cut bacon, a generous helping of macaroni, and onions to go with it. Simple ingredients, but they've all been prepared carefully and properly seasoned. In other words…

"Delicious!"

Red smiles happily when I say that.

∗   ∗   ∗

In the morning, Red had been preparing more medicine, but after lunch he sits at the counter with me. Neither of us is so busy as to need the extra help, so Red said I could take a break, but why would I want to spend less time with him?

"Eh-heh-heh." I have to be careful; looking at him from the side, my mouth just sort slips into a slack smile.

Maybe noticing I was watching him, Red adjusts his clothes just a hair. He has a faded scar that runs from his neck down across his chest. He doesn't normally mind it, but he must have felt a bit awkward when I looked at it. I don't mind it at all, though. It's honestly endearing. Proof of the life he's lived.

It isn't like I enjoy him seeing my scars, either, so I understand the feeling.

"Come on, don't hide it."

But I still want to look.

"H-hey."

"It's fine. It's not the end of the world."

Besides, seeing Red's face blush in embarrassment is a cute side to him entirely different from his usually cool demeanor.

∗   ∗   ∗

Today it's my turn to deliver the fragrance bag to Zeff's sauna.

Zoltan's summers are as hot as ever. Though it's technically already

fall if you go by the calendar. Having grown up in the cool tempera-
tures of Loggervia, part of the reason I chose Zoltan was to live someplace warmer, but I never would have thought it would be this hot.

Once I finish the delivery, I aimlessly walk in the direction of home.

"How can it still be this hot?"

The sun has dropped pretty low in the sky, but it's still warm. I wipe
the sweat on the back of my neck with my bandanna.

"So hot."

All I can do is grumble about it, though.

"Missy," someone calls out to me.

"What do you want?"

I'm already a bit fed up because of the heat, so an edge of annoyance
creeps into my response. But it is what it is. Besides, I'm the uncouth
princess who always sneaked out of the castle. While I might know
proper etiquette, that doesn't mean I like using it.

Turning around, squinting, I see the guy who called out to me looking a little surprised. He's hunched over, his cheeks are sunken, and he
has a dangerous sort of glint in his eyes. I have a vague sense that I've
seen him somewhere before, but I can't place him.

"Do I know you? You need something?"

"Ah, um, I'm a C-rank adventurer by the name of Dir. I had something I wanted to talk with you about."

"Really? Then make it quick."

"It's not really something to discuss in public. Maybe we could head
somewhere to relax and chat over a beer or two?"

"Not interested. See you."

I have the feeling I've met him before somewhere, but the fact that
I've forgotten means he couldn't have been that important. I just
ignore him and start leaving at a brisk pace.

"W-wait a minute!"

"I told you to make it quick."

"Are you sure you want to do that? I know where you hail from."

"It's not like I was particularly hiding anything."

"Not just that. I know your real name, too, Rizlet."

"…Hmph."

"Kh, no need to make such a scary face."

This guy is getting unpleasant, and my ire flares a bit without me realizing.

A look of fear flashes across Dir's face, and then, maybe annoyed at himself for being scared, he makes an arrogant show of spitting on the ground. I furrow my brow at his performance.

"So? Start talking."

"You sure you want to have this conversation out here?"

"You heard me. It's not like I was particularly hiding anything."

"Ha-ha, that's the one and only Rit the hero for you. A true princess does things head-on and in the open, unlike a guy who lives in the shadows, like me." Seeing me reach for my shotel, Dir gets flustered again. "I came to give you a warning."

"About?"

"Don't be so standoffish. Try being a bit nicer, like you are with Red— Gh?!"

I draw my blade, slamming the hilt into his solar plexus. His face pales as he recoils and hunches over. The three people passing nearby glance our way, wondering what's happening.

"I'm a former adventurer. I'm not so high-minded and polite as to laugh it off and forgive someone looking down on me. Got it?"

"Ugh…gh… Y-you asshole…"

"So warn me about what? If you aren't going to talk, I'll just leave."

I feel like beating him down a bit more, but given that I work at an apothecary, maybe I should leave things as they are?

"W-wait a damn minute!"

"What now? If you've got something to say, then quit putting on stupid airs and just spit it out already. You could have saved yourself some pain that way."

"I'll tell Loggervia that you're living with Red."

Hmph, so that's what this is about?

Seeing my quiet response, Dir smirks as he stands back up.

"Heh-heh, cutting loose when you're far from home is all well and good, Princess, but you should realize the position you're in."

"…"

"Put simply, Princess Rizlet, I'd suggest you might want to either stop your little fling with Red and go back to adventuring or else head on home to Loggervia. Hasn't the whole succession problem just about been resolved there now anyway? You're around the age to be getting married off to some tubby old noble, right? 'For the prosperity of both our houses' and all, eh? So sad. But that's the role of a princess, isn't it? I guess it can't be helped. We can't have the princess becoming damaged goods at the hands of some no-name, backwater apothecary, after all."

Perhaps a little mindful of the surroundings, Dir lowers his voice as he prattles. I just heave a disinterested sigh.

"Whoopsie. You're probably better off not trying to take me out here. I've arranged for a letter to be sent to Loggervia immediately in the event that I die."

The gaunt man mistook my sigh for a murderous impulse, I guess. He sure is getting all high-and-mighty talking about what the precautions he's taken. Sheesh… This guy needs to get a grip already.

"Do as you please."

"Huh?"

"Tell my father or whomever else you want," I say before turning on my heel and walking away.

"O-oy! I'm not bluffing here! If Loggervia finds out, you might even get disowned! At best, you're in an awkward position! A hero princess more popular than the prince—you can be sure there are tons of people who would love the chance to be rid of you…"

Man, he's persistent. I decide to delay my return home just a little bit longer.

"You seem to misunderstand, so I'll keep this short and simple. I couldn't care less about my position as Loggervian royalty."

"What?!"

"If it was for Red's sake and to maintain this day-to-day life, I wouldn't mind being disowned as both royalty and a hero. If we can just be Rit and Red in our apothecary, I don't need fame or wealth or anything more than just that."

"Y-you're lying! There's no way your blessing could be satisfied with such an unremarkable life!"

"My blessing? Probably not. But this is what *I* want." I leave and don't look back. Dir must have been dumbfounded; he didn't say another word.

✳   ✳   ✳

The Fire Mage blessing is one of the four main Mage blessings. Its special characteristic is that, in exchange for not being able to use water magic, the skill level required to activate fire magic is lower than for other mages. In addition to that, fire magics with high offensive output can be used at an earlier stage.

One particularly notable difference is that Fireball, which causes an explosion, is a lower-level spell rather than an Intermediate Magic spell as is normally the case. Fire mages are the most popular of the four Mage blessings because, in terms of pure power, they can punch above their level. They are so popular that it was said that even at level one, people with the Fire Mage blessing would not be turned down when trying to join a party.

That's only while everyone's levels are still low, though.

There are a wide variety of offensive spells within the flame magic school. However, that also means that a single kind of energy resistance spell could counter everything a fire mage brings to the table.

Dir the Fire Mage made it as an adventurer for five years. That fifth was the year he was kicked out of his first party. But Dir already understood the peculiarities of his blessing by that point. It granted him a strength that surpassed his level, as long as he faced opponents with a lower level than his own.

The people of this world had a distaste for fighting those not on par with them. Even when goblins attacked a village, it was thought that adventurers of a level similar to the goblins' should be the ones to defeat them.

Blessings developed and grew by fighting and killing opponents who also had a blessing, but if the opponent had a lower blessing level, the efficiency of that growth dropped dramatically. The holy church taught everyone that this was an expression of Demis's will, forbidding the exploitation of weaker people. In a world where good and bad people alike sensed the presence of Demis through their blessing, the holy church's teachings were treated as fact.

But Dir trusted his own blessing over that dogma. He made a living as a mercenary outlaw who pillaged and robbed the weak. Seeing the low-level warriors who protected their small villages being burned to a crisp with no way of resisting evoked a feeling of satisfaction.

The impulses of the Fire Mage blessing led to enjoying seeing things burning in flames. Pillaging a village and then setting it on fire, with the villagers standing there in a daze. All of that triggered a joyous emotion that proved to Dir the correctness of the life he had chosen to live.

"Heh-heh-heh, make a fool of me, will you?"

He was unable to restrain the twitchy grin that crossed his face as he considered what he'd do next.

Dir stood in the shade of the building that neighbored Red & Rit's Apothecary. He had just placed some dried kindling and a vase of oil at the foot of the structure. What for? Arson, of course.

"Ahhh, I'm gonna burn that insolent bitch's happy life to the ground. All because she made a fool of me. Heh-heh!"

Dir had used Shadow Hide, a concealment magic, before starting the preparations for his revenge.

People killed in a fire set like that would not count toward leveling up his blessing, but Dir had successfully killed a knight far more powerful than him using this method in the past. Four other innocent bystanders who'd happened to be staying at the targeted lodge that day had been killed in the blaze, too, but that was a trivial matter to him.

Unfortunately for the would-be arsonist, the person with whom he was dealing this day was not someone who could be fooled by a cloaking spell of that level.

*   *   *

"Hey," I called out to the man about to set fire to my shop.

"Eep?!"

What an irrational guy, just straight-up trying to start a fire like that. I figured someone might try something like this over the thing with Rit but hadn't expected it to go this far.

"If you don't want to get hurt, then don't do anything stupid. Attempted arson's not as serious a crime as going through with it."

Arson was a gravely serious offense. All the more so in the working-class part of Zoltan with so many wooden homes. Even attempted arson would merit a pretty stiff sentence, but actual arson meant death, so it didn't take much to appear light in comparison.

The man in front of me looked around restlessly but smirked when he realized I was alone.

"I heard about you from Ares. You didn't have any real skills and were only in the Hero's party because you were her big brother," he said as he readied himself.

"If you want to have at it, then fine. I'm honestly ticked at you, too."

"Heh-heh, so you remember me?"

"Yeah, you caused more than a few problems in Loggervia."

I knew this man. We had some unfinished business.

I had guessed that the reason Yarandrala and I ended up in the situation with the orcs was because of him getting information out of Ares, but he'd run away before we could know for sure. However, more importantly… Well, it might've been a bit late, but I was still annoyed by the way he'd made a pass at Rit in that bar. He'd put his hand on her shoulder.

I drew my bronze sword and took a step forward. Dir had a Fire Mage blessing. People with Mage blessings tended to have trouble in one-on-ones at close range, but Dir still seemed pretty confident.

When I took another step, Dir's stance faltered slightly. The moon hung at his back.

"It's been awhile since someone was that cautious of me in a fight."

It was almost nostalgic; I'd been getting by as D-rank adventurer here in Zoltan. Honestly, I thought I'd never be in a position like this again. While I was busy awkwardly getting all emotional in the middle of a fight, a nervous smile crossed Dir's face. When I took a third step, Dir's face twisted into a broad smirk.

"Do it now!" Dir shouted, raising his left arm high.

He was looking toward a watchtower that stood in the distance. It would be a great place for a sniper with a bow or crossbow. Yet...nothing happened.

"Huh? Hey! What are you doing?! Shoot already!"

He kept raising his arm over and over, but there was no response.

"This makes it twice now," I said.

Dir's face paled.

"I-it can't be? Not again!"

"The roles are somewhat reversed this time, though."

The reason Rit wasn't around was because she had guessed that Dir would try to get rid of us and had taken a detour to gather some information. While she was gathering intel, she'd heard there had been some two-bit thug adventurer asking around for someone with a Sniper blessing, and just like I had long before, she had preemptively taken care of the problem.

"Grr, damn you!"

Dir started to cast Fireball, but before he could, my sword pierced his shoulder.

"Gah?!"

I hadn't hit a vital point, but it cut to the bone, the pain causing his spell to fail. Concentration was required to activate magic. This was why spells had a disadvantage at close range. Mages could not exhibit their true value without someone there to defend them.

"Ugh! Kh!"

I held my sword pointed at his brow as he recoiled in pain. The vile man toppled back onto the ground. I lowered the blade of my sword to keep it pointed over his head. I only needed the slightest movement to pierce his forehead. It was my win. There was nothing else he could do. Just as I started to put some force into my right hand…

"W-wait!" Dir shouted in a panic. But his next words were not a surrender. "I-if you lay a hand on me, the Thieves Guild won't take it lying down!"

"What?"

"Bighawk thinks you guys are bad for his business! If you kill me, you won't be able to stay in this town!"

"…"

I slowly lowered my weapon.

"Is that so?" I murmured in a low voice.

Dir had committed a grievous mistake. But when he saw my quiet response, he broke out in a triumphant grin.

"Heh-heh-heh, either way, you won't be able to stay here, though. Once you've made an enemy of the Thieves Guild, you can never sleep safe again."

Dir slowly scooted back, still clutching the wound on his shoulder. Then, still acting as though he'd won, he ran away.

"Yeah, it isn't a good idea to make an enemy of the Thieves Guild."

My words never reached Dir as the cowardly fire mage escaped into the night.

*　　　　*　　　　*

I cleaned up the kindling and oil he had left behind. As expected of a fire mage, both were of high quality.

"I'll help myself to the fuel, thanks."

Since Zoltan was surrounded by wetlands, kindling was a bit on the expensive side. I happily reaped the spoils of war. There was something nostalgic about it.

Returning to the house, I put the wood to quick use and lit a fire to prepare a bath. A little while later, Rit returned.

"I'm back!"

"Welcome home."

I met her at the door. For some reason, Rit froze up for a second, and her cheeks turned red.

"What is it?"

"No, it's just, hearing you say 'Welcome home' made me feel really happy all of a sudden."

Hearing her say something like that, there was no way I wouldn't have gotten embarrassed, too.

"H-here, I'll take your cloak, so change into something comfortable."

"S-sure…"

We both smiled clumsily as Rit headed to the bedroom to change.

＊   ＊   ＊

"Here you go."

When she came back, I handed her a cup of hot milk.

"Thank you… Ah, this is delicious; there's honey in it."

"It's a specialty of mine that I made a lot as a kid."

"Coffee's good, but sweet drinks are really nice, too."

That satisfied smile Rit got after eating something delicious overtook her face. It was satisfying enough just watching her in that state. How long had it been since I started thinking about her when I prepared food?

"Something this delicious, I'm going to want to have it again tomorrow."

"All right. I'll make it again tomorrow—and whenever else you want it."

"Hooray!" Rit cheered, looking pleased.

I was just as happy as she was. Making food for her was way more enjoyable than when I was only cooking for myself. That was probably exactly what I wanted out of a slow and easy life.

Epilogue

- - - - - - - - -

Never-Ending Night

"This morning, we received a warning from Rit the hero. Apparently, someone connected to the Thieves Guild was after her. Over the next few days, the guild chief is probably going to be questioning me and the other higher-ups about it. It's got nothing to do with me, of course, but a few favors are going to have to be called in to clear any suspicions. This has been a fiasco."

Bighawk scratched his arm with his thick fingers. Dir was prostrate on the ground in front of him, not daring to say a word.

He couldn't even if he'd wanted to, since he had been gagged. On top of being tied up, every last one of his fingers had also been mercilessly broken to ensure he couldn't use magic.

Dir was crying from the pain and fear, but no one showed any hint of concern for the poor man.

"You probably thought I wouldn't kill you because of whatever valuable secret you know about Rit, but you've got it wrong. You don't understand your position at all."

Dir was trembling, but Bighawk's eyes were cool and merciless.

"That thought is proof you underestimated me. And however valuable that secret you know is, I don't forgive those fool enough to underestimate me."

The large half-orc was the most-feared man in Zoltan. Dir was hit by the realization that he had naively misjudged Bighawk as merely the leader of a bunch of no-name rural thugs, a revelation that had come far too late.

"Take him away."

"Yes sir."

A man lifted the bound Dir over his shoulder.

"Nrgh!!!"

Dir desperately resisted, his frantic eyes pleading for his life.

"Still, everyone makes mistakes. I won't hold it against you forever," Bighawk said with a broad smile.

For just a second, a glimmer of hope shone in Dir's eyes.

"But that will be easy, since I'm never going to see you again." Having said his piece, Bighawk rose and left the room.

"Ngggggggh!!!"

The half-orc did not turn back at Dir's gagged screams.

"What a pity," the man carrying Dir whispered in a sympathetic tone. The thief still did not hesitate to carry Dir down into the blood-spattered room that was the manor's basement.

After that, no one ever saw Dir in Zoltan again.

*   *   *

It was late. The Hero, Ruti, was sitting in her tent, eyes closed as she continued thinking.

Immunity to Sleep was one of the many various immunities and resistances granted by the Hero's blessing. Ruti no longer needed sleep. She could not feel the least bit sleepy. She could maintain a perfect condition twenty-four hours a day without ever having to rest. However, the same was not true of her comrades. She understood that camping for the night was necessary for them.

Still, this is so boring.

The time she spent just sitting there doing nothing was dismally dull.

According to her pet theory, standard resistances and immunities were entirely different things. Standard resistances granted a strength in the face of something, but immunity meant the loss of something. She'd lost the ability to sleep, so her nights were spent like this.

It was better when Big Brother was here, though.

She never felt bored when she could watch him as he slept. Just placing her hand on his chest and feeling his heart beat... She genuinely believed she could endure an eternity if she sat like that with him.

Well, not that she hadn't occasionally snuggled up to him...or maybe nibbled at a finger or his ear or his stomach from time to time. But that was all just trivial playfulness... Yes, that's what she believed.

Ares...

By all rights, even tearing him to pieces would not be enough to satisfy her. However, so long as he did not bear any malice directed at her, she could not lay a hand on a comrade because she was the Hero. The Hero would never injure an ally because of a personal grievance. Her Immunity to Berserk quelled her rage to nothing more than a slight ripple of emotion. Ruti had been robbed of the majority of human emotions and pleasures because of her blessing.

The girl thought back to that time...

✳   ✳   ✳

"Ruti, please hear me out. Your brother has left the party."

That was what Ares had said when he'd visited her room early that morning. Because of her Immunity to Confusion, she'd absorbed what he'd said in a coolheaded manner. The Hero's Immunity to Despair meant she could not be shaken by his words. That was why her response had been just a single word.

"Why?"

"Gideon was self-conscious about his lack of ability and said he would be of more use fighting the demon lord's forces through espionage and guerilla actions than by staying with us. I tried to stop him at first, but he was determined. Eventually, I came to accept the logic of what he was saying. In the end, I decided to see him off with good graces. He left behind his equipment, which we might get some use out of it. He was an admirable man."

"Why you? Why didn't he tell me himself?"

"Probably because he didn't want you to see that side of him, I'd guess. Even though he is far weaker than you, he still tried to comport himself as an older brother to you. A charming bit of conceit. I can certainly understand the sentiment."

I see, so you pushed Big Brother out.

Bursting through the various immunities, Ruti's emotions wavered just a bit.

"Eep?!"

Even that small amount of emotion was enough to elicit a shriek from Ares. The overwhelming pressure Ruti released subconsciously triggered the man's survival instinct. Even so, spurred on by his blessing that he would never hesitate to tell anyone who would listen that he was the most capable of all, he'd taken the action he had decided was best.

Ares gritted his teeth as he put an arm around Ruti's shoulder and hugged her. His heart pounded in terror, and a cold sweat poured down his back. He read back the script he had practiced so many times. The Sage was superior in all ways. No matter the goal, he would accomplish it. The Sage was wise. That was Ares's role.

"I understand the anxiety you might feel at your brother not being here anymore. Before you were the Hero, you were still just a young girl. Compared to the lifetime you've spent with Gideon, our time together has been short, but I will always be your ally."

Even when Ares so clearly overstepped, Ruti could not push him aside. She'd just looked up at him with a cool, fixed, reproachful gaze.

At that moment, though, she sensed someone's presence.

Big Brother?! He was just looking at me! He was just looking at me!! He was just looking at me!!!

The impulses of Divine Blessings resided at the level of thought. But in that moment, Ruti had acted on her human impulse, which occurred preconsciously. Before her brain had processed the information, every inch of her body cried out in despair, and she leaped into action.

"*Ugyhhhhhh?!?!?!*"

Ares's body bent. The noise was less a human voice than the sound of air leaking out of a balloon. The strongest fist in the world had slammed into the man's stomach, pulverizing bones, smashing internal organs, and shredding blood vessels.

The Sage's body slammed into the wall, causing several more bones and organs to lose their shape. Had the VIP room not been reinforced with magic, then even though it had been hit by something as soft as human flesh and blood, even the wall itself would surely have been demolished.

Ares the Sage slumped to the floor, looking like he had been stomped on by a giant dragon.

"Big Brother!"

Ruti wanted to chase after him. To clear up the misunderstanding immediately. But her gaze was focused on Ares, who was on the verge of death. The Hero could not abandon her comrades. Even if the fate of the world was not in the balance, she could not ever abandon anyone, even a truly loathsome person.

Her teeth ground together. The figure disappearing into the distance burned at her nerves. Yet she still falteringly approached Ares.

With the vestiges of consciousness he had left, Ares watched in terror as Ruti approached. She held her hand over him. Thanks to her Healing Hands, Ares, who was at death's door, was restored in the blink of an eye. His broken body had been repaired.

She could no longer sense the presence of her beloved brother. He had run someplace far away. Through her blessing, all the girl could manage to say was…

"I'm sorry."

The Hero gave an apology to the Sage that was completely devoid of feeling. Ares's teeth had chattered as he shuddered in terror.

✳   ✳   ✳

Remembering that moment, the quiver in her heart gave her the slightest bit of pleasure.

It was a memory of one of the few times she had rebelled against the Hero's blessing. Even though it had been only the mildest bitter wave of emotion in her heart that had slipped through all her various immunities, it was a pleasant recollection to her now. Especially because the night provided her with so much free time.

After that day, Ruti had wanted to chase after her brother as soon as possible, but the role of the Hero was to save people in need. Defeating Taraxon, the Demon Lord responsible for so much suffering across the continent, was the top priority.

The Hero's journey had to go on. Because that was what it meant to be the Hero.

"But I need my brother," Ruti whispered softly.

Daybreak was still a long way off.

Afterword

To everyone who has picked up this book, it's a pleasure to meet you. I'm Zappon, a new author.

Just about one month before this book went on sale, I actually debuted with a book published by a different company, so this is my second book. At the time of writing this afterword, my first work has not gone on sale yet, so this afterword has a bit of a "This is my debut work for Sneaker Bunko!" mood to it.

I originally wrote this story for the website Shousetsuka ni Narou. Sneaker Bunko reached out to me with the proposal to adapt it into novel form, and that's why it's able to reach all your hands.

Novelization! By Sneaker Bunko, no less! When I was a kid, in my teenage years (and even now as a no-good adult), there have always been a few Sneaker Bunko light novels on my bookshelf. I'll do my best to make my book something worthy of taking a spot on all your bookshelves, too.

This story has also been serialized as a comic by Ikeno Masahiro in *Monthly Shounen Ace*. The first chapter was published May 26, 2018! Ikeno Masahiro also wrote *Red Dragon*; it's based around the Chu–Han Contention and the era of Xiang Yu and Liu Bang. That story was also published in *Monthly Shonen Ace*. He's also drawn sports and battle manga in other magazines as well. He is an amazing veteran artist who creates wonderful, cool, and cute characters, intense battle scenes, and comical portraits of daily life.

At the time of writing this, the first chapter of the manga has not been finished yet, but the character designs he shared of Rit, Ruti, and the rest were alluring in an entirely different way from those of Yasumo, who handled the illustrations for this book. I can't wait to see them come to life in the manga. If you enjoyed this book, please give the manga a try, too. It will be all the more enjoyable!

Okay, I should leave the happy meandering there and come back to the story of this book. I've loved RPGs for a long time and have played quite a few of them. This work is a story whose main character is a member of the party but drops out partway through.

There are lots of examples in RPGs of characters who leave the party mid-adventure, either because they're just there to help out in the early stages or for other reasons. Whether it's the main character's father, or a first love, or someone who betrayed the party and became an enemy, the separation becomes a turning point in the story and can be one of the most memorable scenes in the game. If any of you reading this afterword are fans of RPGs, perhaps you might have some memories of party members who left the group?

Red, the protagonist of this work, had been given the role of that kind of helper character. This story begins after he had stretched himself a bit too far, having ignored the event where he was supposed to withdraw from the party and continue traveling, only to be finally pushed out. Red's story is one of him receiving no reward for his battles with the demon lord's forces, having all his equipment, weapons, everything, taken away from him, and drifting out to the frontier to find happiness for himself this time around... A totally happy story!

...Yeah. Well, even on the frontier, there are still a few threats, but this is the kind of story where Red and the people around him can nevertheless manage to go about their lives with a smile.

This story was originally published on the Internet, but for it to reach all of your hands in paperback form was thanks to the help of many different people. Yasumo, who gave my characters and their world form. The illustration of Red and Rit in the evening sun was a particular favorite of mine, so I had it printed out to put on display. I would also like to take this chance to thank the designer who arranged the long title to fit so neatly and the proofreaders who pointed out so many typos and misspellings and got this into a state where no company would be ashamed to publish it!

Also, to my editor, Miyakawa, who praised my story, suggested various areas to improve, and worked so hard on so many levels for the sake of this book, from arranging all sorts of meetings to connecting me with the illustrator Yasumo. It is an honor to have my story added to the list of projects you've managed. Thank you very much.

And also, thanks to all the readers who supported the web version of this story. Were it not for you, this book would never have existed in the first place.

Lastly, I would like to thank all of you who picked up this novel. If I was able to provide an enjoyable experience worthy of putting this volume on your bookshelf, then there is nothing more gratifying to me as an author.

Let's meet again in the second book!

Zappon
2018, around when the cherry blossoms began to fall

Nice to meet you.
This is Yasumo.
All of the
characters had
such vivid
personalities
that it was a
pleasure to
draw them.
I hope I could
convey at least
a little bit of
their allure!

There's a lot of strife in the world, but they're still living their slow and easy life.

BANISHED
FROM THE
HERO'S PARTY,
I Decided to Live a Quiet Life in the Countryside

2

COMING 2021!